VAMPIRE NURSE

The Crimson Veil

DRAVEN P. SLOUTI

ISBN:
Paperback 978-1-966890-13-3
eBook 978-1-966890-14-0
Audiobook 978-1-966890-15-7

Azalea City Publishing, LLC
Mobile, AL 36693
www.azaleacitypublishing.com
Cover design: Artillery Design Company Ltd
https://www.artillerydesign.co

DEDICATION

To Cheryl. Thank you for your vampiric efforts to save what is left of my foot.

ACKNOWLEDGEMENTS

Thank you to Brian Lambrect, Deza Rae Collins, and Roni Chaudron for reading this work and giving me feedback. Your help is appreciated more than words can express.

Thank you to Cheryl Booth for inspiring this story and all the work you have done over the last year, including encouraging me not to give up.

Chapter 1

Night Shift

In the heart of St. Augustine's Hospital, where neo-Gothic spires pierce the moonlit sky, a labyrinth of secrets lies buried beneath the sterile halls. The hospital, a towering edifice of stone and shadow, looms over the city like a silent sentinel, its ancient catacombs whispering tales of forgotten souls and hidden horrors.

Evelyn Carter, a new nurse on the graveyard shift, navigates the fluorescent-lit corridors with a mix of apprehension and excitement. Her first week at St. Augustine's has been a whirlwind of adjustment, but the anonymity of the night shift suits her newfound nature perfectly. As a vampire, recently turned during a car-crash rescue that left her teetering on the brink of death, Evelyn finds solace in the shadows.

The hospital, with its century-old catacombs, hums with an energy that Evelyn can barely comprehend, a pulsating heartbeat of the past, resonating through the present. As the clock strikes midnight, the fluorescent lights begin to flicker, casting eerie shadows across the walls. Rain lashes against the windows, its rhythm a haunting melody that accompanies the hospital's secrets. Evelyn, attuned to the hospital's whispers, knows that tonight is a night of revelation.

In the depths of the catacombs, ancient tombs hold more than just the remains of the long-dead. They hold a power that has been dormant for centuries, a power that Evelyn has only just begun to understand. As a new vampire, she is both a guardian and a seeker of this power, a delicate balance between her immortal nature and her mortal duty.

The hospital's corridors, usually bustling with activity, are now eerily quiet, the silence broken only by the distant hum of machinery and the occasional creak of the building settling into the night. Evelyn moves through the shadows, her senses heightened, her mind focused on the task ahead.

The night unfolds like a tapestry, weaving together the threads of Evelyn's past and present, her duty and her desire. In the shadows of St. Augustine's Hospital, where the lines between life and death blur, Evelyn must confront the secrets that lie within her own heart and the ancient power that beckons her from the depths of the catacombs. As she embarks on this journey, she realizes that her new life as a vampire is just beginning, and the mysteries of the hospital are only the first chapter in her eternal tale.

As Evelyn approaches a patient's room, her mind is a whirlwind of thoughts, a strict routine that she has meticulously maintained since her transformation. Her thoughts are a constant companion, a voice that guides her through the complexities of her new existence.

"Check the animal-blood packs," she reminds herself, her fingers brushing against the cool metal of the refrigerator where she stores her sustenance. The packs, neatly labeled and arranged, are a testament to her discipline. She knows the importance of maintaining her strength, especially during these long nights.

"Contact lenses," she whispers, her reflection in the mirror revealing eyes that glow with an otherworldly light. With a practiced hand, she inserts the lenses, dulling the intensity of her gaze. The transformation is subtle, but it allows her to blend into the shadows, unnoticed by her colleagues and patients.

"Mints," she adds, popping a fresh one into her mouth. The cool, minty flavor masks the lingering taste of blood, a reminder of her true nature. It's a small comfort, a way to maintain a semblance of normalcy in a world that has become increasingly strange.

As she stands in the corridor, her thoughts drift to the man in the room before her. His affliction resonates with her. She wonders if she can maintain control of her thirst.

Evelyn's heart races as she steps into the room, the fluorescent lights flickering once more. The man in the bed stirs, his eyes meeting hers with an intensity that sends shivers down her spine.

"Who are you?" she asks, her voice barely above a whisper. The man's lips curve into a ghostly smile, and he reaches out, his fingers brushing against hers. The touch is electric, a jolt of energy that courses through her veins.

Evelyn's mind races, her thoughts a jumbled mix of curiosity and apprehension. She knows that this encounter is more than just a chance meeting, that it is a test of her strength. As she leans closer, her eyes locked with his, she realizes that her journey as a vampire is only just beginning, and the mysteries of this new life are waiting to be unraveled.

The calm of the night is shattered as the sound of rushing footsteps and urgent voices echoes through the corridor. Evelyn's head snaps up, her senses immediately heightened. A trauma patient is being wheeled into her ward, the copper scent of blood heavy in the air. Her fangs ache, and a haze of hunger begins to cloud her vision. She takes a deep breath, her mind racing as she fights the primal urge that threatens to overwhelm her.

"Focus," she whispers to herself, recalling the meditation techniques taught by her mysterious sire. The absence of this enigmatic figure, who turned her and then vanished, haunts her every moment. His teachings, however, remain a lifeline, a way for her to maintain control in the face of her most basic instincts.

Her meditation techniques are a blend of ancient rituals and modern mindfulness, designed to harness the power of her newfound vampiric senses. She visualizes a shimmering, ethereal mist, a calming veil that she draws around herself, a shield against the all-consuming hunger. The mist, a silvery blue, swirls with the rhythm of her heartbeat, pulsing with a soothing, hypnotic energy.

As she inhales, Evelyn imagines the mist seeping into her pores, cooling her blood, quenching the fire of her thirst. With each exhale, she releases the tension, the mist carrying away the primal urges that threaten to overwhelm her. Her mind's eye focuses on a single, serene image, a tranquil lake at dusk, the water still and reflective, mirroring the calm she seeks within.

She imagines a series of mental locks, each one a barrier against the scent of blood. She begins with her senses, locking away the heightened smell, then the sharpness of sight, and finally, the acute hearing. Each lock clicks into place with a mental command, a whisper in the depths of her mind: "Lock sight, lock sound, lock scent."

In the stillness of her meditation, Evelyn finds a moment of peace, a respite from the storm of her vampiric nature. The mist settles, and she emerges from her trance, her eyes clear, her control restored. It is a reprieve, a reminder of the power she holds within, and the strength she must summon to navigate the shadows of her new life.

Evelyn steps forward, her movements fluid and precise as she approaches the patient. The orderly, Mateo Alvarez, flashes her a friendly, flirtatious smile, his dark eyes sparkling with a mix of concern and admiration. "Another wild night, huh?" he says, his voice a soothing balm amidst the chaos. Evelyn offers him a small, grateful smile, her hands steady as she takes over the patient's care.

Dr. Meredith Kwon, the sharp-eyed attending physician, arrives on the scene, her presence commanding and reassuring. "Evelyn, what do we have here?" she asks, her gaze flicking between the patient and the nurse with a keen, assessing look. Evelyn quickly provides the details, her voice steady despite the storm raging inside her.

"Arterial bleeding, likely from a work accident. BP is dropping, and we need to stabilize him ASAP," Evelyn reports, her professionalism a shield against the hunger that gnaws at her. Dr. Kwon nods, her movements efficient as she begins to direct the team, her eyes never leaving the patient.

As they work together, Evelyn feels a strange sense of belonging, a connection to her fading mortal life. Mateo's friendly banter and Dr. Kwon's steady leadership ground her, reminding her of the humanity she still holds within. The patient's condition stabilizes, and the immediate crisis passes, but the scent of blood lingers, a constant test of her resolve.

Evelyn steps back, her breath ragged as she fights the last vestiges of the hunger haze. She knows that she must return to her duties, but the encounter has left her shaken, her thoughts a whirlwind of questions and doubts. As she walks away, the fluorescent lights flickering overhead, she can't help but wonder what secrets the night still holds, and how she will navigate the delicate balance between her immortal nature and her mortal duty. In the shadows of St. Augustine's Hospital, Evelyn finds solace in the relationships she has forged, knowing that they are the anchor that keeps her tethered to the world of the living.

Chapter 2

Whispers of the Hunt

Downtown Crescent City never truly slept. It only shifted like a restless dream between the shimmer of daylight and the pulse of its humid nights. The gas lamps along Royal Street burned low, their glass chimneys fogged with the breath of magnolia and salt. Beyond them, the harbor murmured against the stone embankment, whispering secrets to the tide.

The air was heavy enough to taste, thick with the sweetness of flowers and the faint tang of rust and blood that came from the iron balconies and the sea. Crickets sang beneath the weight of the heat, and somewhere a jazz saxophone bent a lonely note into the dark, letting it curl between the narrow alleys and overgrown courtyards.

Crescent City had an old soul. Its buildings leaned into one another like conspirators, their shutters sagging with stories too long kept. The cobblestones remembered the steps of sailors, sinners, and saints. And of creatures who belonged to none of them. Beneath the glow of the lamps, shadows moved where no footsteps fell.

Tonight, the moon was a tarnished coin above the bay, and the city waited for something it could not name.

The television in the staff lounge flickered against the dull green walls, its glow fighting the hum of fluorescent lights and the low whir of an aging vending machine. Evelyn sat on the edge of a plastic chair, her scrubs clinging slightly to her skin in the humid air. Her coffee had gone cold an hour ago, but she lifted the cup anyway. More for the comfort of the motion than the taste.

Onscreen, the local anchor's voice was smooth and detached, as if distance could sanitize the horror.

"Police are investigating the discovery of a body near the old river docks late last night. Authorities say the victim suffered extensive injuries. Unconfirmed reports suggest the throat was…"

The anchor hesitated, her polished smile faltering for half a heartbeat.

"…torn out. Officials have not ruled out the possibility of a ritual killing."

Evelyn's hand stilled halfway to her mouth.

"Jesus," murmured Lila, the charge nurse, from the corner. She stood by the snack machine, arms crossed, eyes fixed on the screen. "That's the second one this month."

"Third," Evelyn corrected softly. She set the cup down, its plastic rim scraping against the tabletop. "The dockworker two weeks ago. They never found who did it."

"They won't," Lila said. "Half the precinct's afraid to go down there after dark." She gave a short, humorless laugh. "Can't say I blame them."

The anchor moved on to the weather, promising rain that would always come. Evelyn stared at the muted commercials that followed, lost in the static shimmer of the screen.

"You okay, Ev?" Lila asked, tearing open a bag of chips.

"Yeah." Evelyn blinked, forcing a smile. "Just tired."

But that wasn't true. What she felt wasn't fatigue. It was a pull, low and insistent, like something in her bones had stirred at the mention of blood and moonlight on the river.

Outside the staff lounge window, the lamps of Crescent City burned steadily in the haze, and somewhere beyond them, the tide whispered against the docks.

The staff lounge door swung open with a squeak of tired hinges and the faint scent of antiseptic and cheap cologne.

"If I don't get a night off soon, I'm filing for emotional damages," Mateo said, stepping in with his usual lopsided grin. His dark curls were damp from the humidity, his ID badge dangling askew. "What'd I miss? Someone finally win the lottery?"

Lila snorted. "Close. Another body down by the docks."

Mateo froze mid-step, grin faltering. "You're kidding."

Evelyn shook her head. "News says it happened last night. Throat torn out."

He let out a low whistle, dragging a chair backward with one hand before sinking into it. "That's messed up. Sounds like something out of a horror movie."

"A *ritual killing*," Lila added, air-quoting with her fingers. "At least, that's what they're calling it now. Guess it sells better than 'unsolved murder.'"

Mateo leaned forward, elbows on his knees, eyes flicking between them. "You think it's the same guy as before?"

"Could be," Evelyn said quietly. "Same area. Same kind of wounds."

"Man," Mateo muttered, shaking his head. "I used to hang out down there for open mic nights. Guess I'll skip that for a while." He forced a smile. "Not that I'm afraid of the dark or anything."

Lila rolled her eyes. "Sure you're not."

Evelyn's lips twitched. "We could test that. Go check the docks after shift, see how brave you really are."

Mateo gave a mock shiver. "I'd rather face Mrs. Delacroix in Room 214 again. She threw her urinal at me *twice* last night."

Lila laughed, but the sound faded quickly under the drone of the air vent. The silence that followed felt too still, as though the city outside was holding its breath.

Then, from the corner of the room, the old police scanner crackled to life. It's static hiss slicing through the quiet.

A male voice came through, warped and thin with interference.

"units in the vicinity of Riverfront and Dauphine, possible…"

The rest dissolved into static, a burst of white noise that prickled along Evelyn's spine.

Mateo frowned, glancing toward the machine. "That thing even still work?"

Lila stood slowly, chip bag forgotten. "It shouldn't. Nobody's used it since the hurricane knocked the tower out."

The scanner crackled again, louder this time.

"Repeat, officer down. Requesting backup at…"

The transmission cut, leaving only the hum of the lights and the soft clatter of Evelyn's heartbeat in her ears.

She met Mateo's gaze. His grin was gone.

The scanner spat another burst of static, then caught on a frequency that sounded almost human..

"Unit… seven… inbound… delta pattern… confirm…"

Evelyn froze. That phrasing, *delta pattern*. It clawed at something buried deep in her memory, something that smelled of iron and candle smoke and blood.

"There it goes again," Mateo said, standing and giving the machine a cautious look. "Swear to God, that thing's been dead since 2018. We only keep it around because nobody wants to toss it."

Lila tilted her head, frowning. "Maybe it's picking up dispatch from the county line? Or some trucker frequency?"

Evelyn shook her head slowly. "No… that's not police code."

"You'd know?" Mateo teased, trying for lightness but not quite getting there.

"Maybe," she said quietly.

The scanner crackled once more, voices overlapping in a low, rhythmic cadence.

"…north pier secure… mark the circle… repeat, mark the circle…"

Evelyn's stomach knotted. The words tumbled against the edge of recognition, pulling up memories she had spent too much time trying to forget: the hiss of Latin invocations, the gleam of silver under candlelight, her sire's voice whispering from the dark.

If you ever hear the circle spoken in the open air, you run, child. Hunters never use it unless blood's already been spilled.

The sound distorted again, a long metallic shriek.

"What circle?" Lila asked, her voice low now.

"Probably some code for containment," Mateo said quickly, though his laugh was hollow. "SWAT lingo or whatever."

Evelyn didn't answer. Her gaze stayed fixed on the scanner as her eyes started to glow bright under her contacts, its red light flickering like a heartbeat.

"Unit Seven to Base, confirmation, target confirmed. Eyes on the nest. Repeat… eyes on the nest."

This time, Evelyn's breath caught audibly.

"Nest?" Lila echoed. "Like… what, birds?"

Evelyn rose from her chair, every muscle in her body tight. "No," she whispered. "Not birds."

The scanner hissed louder now, insistent, as if it were trying to force its way back to life after years of silence.

Mateo swallowed hard. "Evelyn… what the hell is going on?"

She didn't answer him either. Her glowing eyes were on the flickering screen, but her thoughts were miles away, down by the docks where the night still breathed heavy with magnolia and death.

The scanner kept murmuring in broken phrases; half lost to static, half alive with intent.

"...secondary target confirmed... authorization granted... cleanse and contain..."

Evelyn flinched at the last word. *Cleanse.* The hunters always used that one. Never *kill.* Never *murder.* It sounded righteous that way.

She could feel her pulse quicken, though her kind hadn't needed a heartbeat in years. Fear crawled cold and electric under her skin, but something hotter followed close behind. Anger.

"Evelyn?" Mateo's voice was cautious now. "You're looking a little pale."

"Yeah," Lila added softly. "You okay?"

Evelyn forced her eyes away from the scanner, meeting theirs. "They're not police," she said.

Mateo frowned. "Who then?"

"Hunters."

Lila blinked. "Hunters? Like… , bounty hunters?"

Evelyn hesitated. The word *vampire* sat sharp and bitter on her tongue, impossible to speak. She pressed her lips together instead.

"Not exactly," she murmured.

The scanner hissed again, a rush of static followed by another clipped voice.

"Alpha team, maintain visual. Civilians nearby, non-discriminatory protocol authorized."

That did it. Evelyn's hands clenched into fists. The paper cup on the table collapsed under her grip, cold coffee spilling across the Formica in a slow brown spread.

"Non-discriminatory," she said through her teeth. "They never learn. Doesn't matter who we are, what we do, if they think they've found a nest, they burn it all."

Mateo blinked. "*We?*"

She caught herself, jaw tightening. "Them. I meant them."

Lila gave her a long, uncertain look, but said nothing.

The air felt too thick now, pressing close, alive with the scent of ozone and magnolia drifting in through the cracked window. Evelyn could almost hear her sire's voice again:

Hunters kill the feral because they fear them. But they kill us, too, because we remind them it's not the hunger that's monstrous, it's the choice.

The scanner popped once more, as though mocking her silence.

"Visual confirmed. Approaching structure now... prepare ignition."

Mateo stared at it, then at her. "Ignition? What are they talking about?"

Evelyn's chair scraped back against the tile. Her voice was a whisper edged with panic. "They're going to torch something."

Her eyes darted to the window, out toward the dark stretch of riverfront where the lamps flickered like dying stars.

"And if they're right about what's down there," she said, "they won't care who burns with it."

Evelyn stood motionless as the scanner went silent again, leaving only the hum of the fluorescent lights and the faint drip of coffee from the table's edge. Her hands trembled, and she tucked them into her pockets to hide it.

Lila broke the stillness first.

"Maybe it's nothing," she said. "Some kind of hoax. That thing's ancient…"

"No," Evelyn interrupted softly. "It's real."

She could still hear the coded phrases echoing in her head; *mark the circle, cleanse and contain.* Hunters never broadcast openly unless they meant to make a point. Fear was half their weapon.

Mateo shifted uneasily. "If it is real… shouldn't we, I don't know, call somebody?"

Evelyn gave a bitter laugh. "Who would believe it? Cops won't. Reporters won't. And if the wrong people do, someone else ends up dead."

She turned toward the window, pressing her palm to the cool glass. Outside, Crescent City shimmered under its veil of heat and haze. Somewhere in that sprawl of alleyways and abandoned warehouses, others like her were hiding and feeding quietly, keeping their heads down, pretending at humanity because it was safer that way.

She had stayed away from them since she was turned. It was easier not to care, easier not to risk exposure or worse, the pull of belonging that always came with it. Her sire had taught her that isolation was survival. But tonight, with the echo of hunter code still ringing in her ears, the old rules felt suddenly fragile.

If they find the nest…

Evelyn shut her eyes. She could picture their faces even now. Those few she'd glimpsed in backroom bars and shadowed corners, their eyes catching the light just a little too long. Strangers, all of them.

"You okay, Ev?" Mateo asked, quieter this time.

"Yeah," she said, though her voice trembled on the word. "Just thinking."

"About what?"

She hesitated. Then, softly: "Whether to stay quiet... or warn them."

Lila frowned. "Warn who?"

Evelyn turned from the window. "No one you'd ever meet." Her smile was faint, haunted. "At least, not in daylight."

The scanner hissed once more like a dying breath then went dead completely.

Evelyn stood there for a long moment, listening to the silence it left behind. In that hollow quiet, the weight of choice pressed hard against her ribs: fear on one side, the flicker of something dangerously like hope on the other.

Outside, the night exhaled thick with magnolia, sea-salt, and the first scent of rain.

Chapter 3

The Arrival

The trauma bay hummed with the peculiar electricity of midnight emergencies; the rhythmic hiss of oxygen lines and the low buzz of fluorescent lights that had seen too many long nights.

Evelyn moved quickly between curtained bays, her scrubs damp at the collar, her thoughts frayed thin. The metallic scent of antiseptic clung to everything, sharp enough to sting her senses, but beneath it was something else, ozone.

The storm was close. She could feel it pressing against the hospital's steel and glass, thickening the air until every breath felt like it carried a charge. Outside, thunder rolled low over the Gulf, shaking the windows in their frames.

"Carter, I need another unit of O-neg!" Dr. Rollins barked across the room.

"On it," Evelyn replied automatically, snatching the blood bag from the cooler and handing it off to the nurse at the bedside. The patient was a young man in his mid-twenties who lay pale and unconscious beneath a tangle of IV lines and surgical drapes.

She caught a whiff of his blood as they hooked the line. For an instant, her throat tightened, that hunger flaring in a flash of crimson memory. She forced it down, biting the inside of her cheek until she tasted iron.

"Vitals stabilizing," the monitor announced in its mechanical voice.

Evelyn stepped back, steadying herself. Around her, the ER pulsed with its usual chaos. However, tonight it all felt… sharper. Closer.

Every sound carried a hum beneath it, like the static she'd heard earlier through the scanner. The words she couldn't forget: *mark the circle. cleanse and contain.*

"You good, Carter?" Mateo's voice cut through the noise. He'd appeared at her elbow again, gloves on, smile faint but genuine.

"Fine," she said, not quite meeting his eyes.

He followed her gaze toward the storm-lashed windows. "You sure? You look like you've seen a ghost."

"Maybe I have," she murmured.

He frowned, about to press, but the intercom crackled overhead, a sharp burst of static before the nurse's voice came through:

"Incoming trauma, ETA five minutes. Male, late thirties, found near the river docks."

Evelyn's heart stopped cold.

Mateo exhaled a curse. "Another one? What the hell's going on down there?"

Thunder rolled again, this time closer, right above the building, rattling the metal cabinets. Evelyn's pulse picked up, her body moving before her thoughts could catch up.

"I'll prep Bay Three," she said, voice tight.

As she pulled on a fresh pair of gloves, lightning flashed outside, painting the room in white-blue light. For an instant, the world felt suspended and utterly still.

And in that silence, Evelyn couldn't shake the feeling that the storm wasn't just weather. It was a warning.

The double doors burst open under the red glare of the emergency lights. Rain and wind slammed in behind the gurney as two paramedics pushed it through the entrance, their voices overlapping in clipped urgency.

"Male, late thirties, possible crush injuries, multiple lacerations, unresponsive since extraction!"

The metallic tang of blood hit thick in the air immediately. Evelyn's senses flared in protest. It wasn't human blood. It was colder and darker.

Dr. Rollins stepped in beside her. "What's his name?"

"ID says *Lucian Devereaux*," one of the medics answered, panting. "Warehouse collapse near the old docks. A whole wall came down on him. EMS says no pulse for five minutes, but then…"

The medic hesitated, glancing at his partner.

"Then what?" Rollins snapped.

"Then he *moved*. Sat up on his own before we loaded him. We… uh… sedated him."

Mateo muttered, "Well, that's not creepy at all."

Evelyn stepped forward, her eyes narrowing on the patient. Lucian's skin was pale and almost translucent, but not with the sickly tone of blood loss. It was marble and flawless, even through the cuts that scored his arms and chest. Cuts that should have closed by now.

She reached for a gauze pad, pressing it gently to one of the wounds. The blood soaked through instantly, still flowing, refusing to clot.

Dr. Rollins frowned. "Pressure dressing. Now."

"Already tried," one of the medics said. "It's like the blood won't stick. Never seen anything like it."

Evelyn's pulse quickened. She had. She'd *felt* that same cold stasis in her own body after feeding, when her veins hummed with borrowed life. Whatever Lucian was, or whoever, he wasn't entirely human.

A low groan escaped him then, soft and hoarse. His head turned on the gurney, damp hair clinging to his face. His eyes fluttered open, gray as storm light.

For an instant, Evelyn felt the room narrow around her, the world condensing to that single, impossible gaze.

"Vitals dropping," the monitor blared.

Rollins barked orders, "Epi ready! Charge to 200!" but the voice felt distant to Evelyn now, like an echo underwater.

Lucian's lips moved; cracked and bloodied. The words barely carried over the storm outside.

"The circle… they found it…"

Evelyn's breath caught. "What did you say?"

His eyes flicked to her, focusing for a heartbeat. Then he whispered, *"Hunter fire."*

The lights flickered with the next crash of thunder, and for a heartbeat, the whole trauma bay plunged into darkness.

When they came back, Lucian's hand was wrapped around her wrist. His grip was cold, strong, desperate.

"You shouldn't be here," he rasped. "They're coming."

Evelyn froze, Lucian's cold hand still gripping her wrist. The room around her blurred with voices muffled and movement slowed, as something unseen rippled through the air between them.

It began as a faint vibration, a subtle pulse beneath the hum of the flights. Then it deepened, low and resonant until it thrummed through her bones like the echo of a buried chord.

His *aura*.

She could feel it radiating off him in dark and intense waves. The kind of presence that bent the air itself. It wasn't hunger, not exactly. It was older than that. Older than either of them should have been.

Her own instincts rose in response, uncoiling like a living thing inside her. The fine hairs on her arms stood on end. Beneath the sterile stink of antiseptic and metal, she caught it: the faint sweetness of ancient blood.

"Evelyn!" Rollins barked from somewhere to her left. "Step back! We're losing him!"

But she couldn't move. Her body refused. Every cell screamed at her to stay still, to listen to him.

The hum deepened, turning electric. Lightning flashed outside, flooding the trauma bay with white light, and for a heartbeat, she saw him not as the broken figure on the gurney, but as something whole, something vast and terrible cloaked in shadow and rain.

And beneath the instinctive fear, something else stirred. Recognition.

Not memory, it was something older than memory. Like a scent carried on smoke.

Lucian's eyes flickered open again, the stormlight catching silver in their depths. His voice was barely more than a vibration against her skin.

"You feel it too."

Evelyn swallowed hard. "What are you?"

He almost smiled, blood curling at the edge of his lips. "Not what. *Who.*"

The monitor screamed. Flatline.

"Clear!" Rollins shouted, grabbing the defibrillator paddles.

Evelyn stumbled back at last, breaking the connection. The hum vanished, leaving her cold and hollow.

As the charge built and the paddles hit Lucian's chest, thunder crashed so loud it rattled the glass.

And somewhere, beneath the storm, Evelyn could still feel the ghost of that resonance trembling in her bones.

"Got a pulse!" one of the nurses shouted as the monitor spiked back to life, the steady rhythm of beeps echoing through the chaos.

Dr. Rollins exhaled hard, wiping his brow. "Good. Keep it steady. Let's start a transfusion; he's lost too much blood. Carter, get another unit of O-neg, wide open."

Evelyn blinked, still half caught in the echo of Lucian's aura. "Doctor…"

"Now, Carter!"

Her body obeyed before her mind did. She tore open the cooler, hands moving on muscle memory as she spiked the line and hung the fresh bag. Red fluid began to snake down the tubing, drop by deliberate drop.

Lucian stirred on the gurney, his breath catching. The monitors flickered again.

"BP's dropping!" one of the nurses said. "Eighty over fifty and falling!"

Rollins swore under his breath. "He's crashing again! Get the second unit ready!"

But Evelyn's eyes were locked on the transfusion line. The blood, *human blood,* wasn't entering his veins. It hung there, quivering, as if the tubing itself resisted the flow. Then, abruptly, the line darkened.

Lucian's body convulsed once, muscles tightening under the sheets. His back arched, veins rising black and sharp beneath his skin. The heart monitor screamed into chaos.

"He's rejecting it!" Evelyn said sharply.

"Impossible!" Rollins barked, grabbing the IV line. "It's universal donor… there's no reaction type…"

Lucian's eyes snapped open. The storm outside answered in a burst of thunder that rattled the light fixtures. The blood in the line reversed course, surging *backward* toward the bag in a pulsing shudder before bursting from the port in a misted spray.

The entire trauma bay froze.

Lucian slumped back against the gurney, trembling. His breathing slowed to something eerily measured. The color returned to his face not as life, but as something colder, deliberate.

Dr. Rollins stood rigid, staring at the red streaks spattered across his gloves. "What the hell was that?"

Mateo's voice was hushed. "That's… that's not normal."

Evelyn forced her feet to move, stepping closer to the gurney. Her voice came low, steady. "Doctor, the transfusion's overloading his system. He's stabilizing without it."

Rollins blinked at her, dazed. "Without… it? He lost half his blood volume, Carter!"

Lucian's eyes met hers again. That same low hum coiled faintly through her bones, quieter this time, like a shared secret.

"No," he rasped, voice raw. "Not lost. Not mine."

Rollins turned sharply. "What did he say?"

Evelyn didn't answer. She couldn't. Because deep down, beneath the clinical chaos and fluorescent glare, she knew exactly what he meant.

The blood wasn't his. It had never been.

The chaos in the trauma bay began to ebb. The alarms quieted, replaced by the steady rhythm of the heart monitor; slow and deliberate. Almost impossible. Lucian lay utterly still, his breath even, his skin no longer the deathly gray it had been minutes ago.

Dr. Rollins tore off his gloves, still staring at the blood-spattered floor. "Get a full panel started. Type and cross again, just in case. I want imaging, a full workup. A full trauma protocol."

Evelyn didn't respond. Her focus was on Lucian. On the faint rise and fall of his chest. On the stillness that wasn't sleep.

Lightning flashed outside, bathing the room in pale blue light. For an instant, she saw it: a mark over his heart, half-hidden beneath blood and gauze. Not a wound. A *scar*.

It was shaped like a crest; delicate, almost sigil-like, the lines fine and intricate as if etched beneath the skin. As she watched, it pulsed once, twice; a faint shimmer, as though it were inked with light instead of pigment. Then it stilled again.

Evelyn's throat went dry. No one else seemed to notice. The others were busy cleaning, resetting, murmuring orders and numbers that blurred into meaningless noise.

She reached forward, fingertips hovering just above the mark, feeling the faint heat radiating from it. The pulse there was not human. It was deeper. Like the echo she'd felt in her bones before, resonating in a language older than breath.

Lucian's lips parted slightly, a whisper caught between words. She leaned in without meaning to, the storm rumbling low against the windows.

"The circle is broken," he breathed.

Her heart gave a single, hard thud.

"Carter!" Rollins called sharply. "Stay with us. Prep him for transfer to ICU."

She straightened quickly, mask slipping back into place. "Yes, Doctor."

As she moved to help, she glanced one last time at Lucian. The mark over his heart had faded to nothing but a faint shadow, as though it had never been there.

But Evelyn could still feel it. That low, resonant hum. That unspoken pull between them.

Outside, thunder rolled again, and the rain began in earnest. Like a steady drumming against the hospital glass, washing the blood from the city streets.

And beneath the storm's rising voice, Evelyn Carter couldn't shake the feeling that Crescent City was holding its breath; waiting for something to wake.

Chapter 4

First Taste

The power flickered once , twice, then the world went dark.

For a heartbeat, the ER fell silent except for the distant hiss of the storm outside. Then the generator kicked in with a guttural hum, bathing the supply corridor in harsh red light. It strobed in uneven bursts, throwing long, skeletal shadows against the walls and shelves.

Evelyn stood at the end of the corridor, one hand braced on a metal cart, watching the lights pulse like a dying heartbeat. The air smelled of antiseptic and ozone, sharp and metallic, as if the storm itself had seeped into the hospital's veins.

She'd come here to breathe, *pretend* she still could, after helping transfer Lucian upstairs. But the red light made the walls feel too close, too alive.

Every flicker sent her reflection flashing in the glass of the supply cabinets: pale skin, dark eyes, pupils a fraction too wide. For a moment, she thought she saw someone else staring back. A ghost of herself from long ago, the version that had promised never to get involved again.

But then she heard it.

A low hum, faint but familiar; not mechanical. Resonant. The same vibration that had rolled through her bones when Lucian's hand had closed around her wrist. It drifted down the corridor like a memory, tugging at her senses.

She turned toward the sound, pulse quickening. The supply door at the far end stood slightly ajar, its red emergency light blinking behind the glass window like an unseen heartbeat.

Her rational mind told her it was nothing; the generator was cycling, perhaps the ICU backup grid was coming online. However, the part of her that belonged to the night, the one she kept locked behind blood and discipline, whispered otherwise.

He's awake.

The thought came unbidden, unwelcome. Yet it sank into her like truth.

She hesitated, hand hovering over the door handle. Behind her, the corridor buzzed faintly with static. The sound of the old police scanner crackling again from the lounge, though it shouldn't have been on.

For a moment, Evelyn stood between the two sounds, the hum of something ancient in front of her, and the coded chatter of hunters in the distance.

And somewhere in that narrow space of red light and storm-shadow, she realized she couldn't hide from either anymore.

A sharp crash split through the corridor.

Evelyn jumped, spinning toward the sound. One of the patient bays near the end of the hall burst open, a nurse stumbling backward as a gurney jolted against the doorframe. The red generator light strobed again, turning everything into flashes of motion: white coats, tangled tubing, and the gleam of metal and glass.

"Dammit! he pulled the line!" the nurse cried.

Evelyn was already moving. She pushed through the doorway, instincts overriding thought. The patient on the gurney thrashed weakly, his arm slick with blood where the IV catheter had ripped free. The saline stand toppled over, the IV line snapping as the bag burst against the floor.

A warm spray of blood hit her cheek, spattering across her mask and neck.

For a moment, she froze, the scent flooding her senses, still human. Her fangs ached beneath her lips, sharp enough to cut through restraint.

"Carter, hold him still!" someone shouted.

Evelyn blinked, the haze breaking. "On it."

She grabbed the man's wrist, pinning it firmly as another nurse pressed gauze to the wound. Her hands shook, not from fear, but from the unbearable awareness of the pulse beating beneath his skin.

It had been months since she'd fed from the vein. She told herself she didn't want to anymore. However, the scent was overwhelming, filling the small bay with warmth that drowned out the metallic bite of antiseptic.

The generator lights flickered again, casting everything in a slow, pulsing red glow. The patient moaned. Evelyn's heartbeat answered in kind, a rhythm she shouldn't have had.

"Pressure's holding," the nurse said, breathless.

Evelyn released the patient's wrist, stepping back quickly, forcing her breath to steady. She could feel blood cooling on her skin beneath the mask.

"You okay?" Mateo's voice came from the doorway, his silhouette framed in red.

She nodded, maybe too fast. "Just startled."

He glanced at her face. "You're bleeding."

"Not mine," she said.

The lights flickered once more. The hum of the generator dipped low, then recovered with a guttural growl. For a heartbeat, in the momentary dark, Evelyn thought she heard something else under the sound, a voice.

Soft. Familiar. *"You shouldn't be near blood right now."*

The scent clung to her.

Evelyn scrubbed at her skin with alcohol wipes in the supply corridor, but it only spread the smell sweet and *alive.* Her gloves were gone, her mask discarded in the sink, but the warmth of the blood lingered beneath her nails, seeping into her pores.

She could still *taste* it in the air.

The scent hit her again, stronger this time, a wave of warmth carried on the recycled air from the trauma bay. The patient's blood, fresh and human, It crawled beneath her skin, sank into her throat, and burned behind her eyes.

Her control shattered.

The pulse of red light, the rhythm of rain against the glass windows to the outside world, all of it blurred into a single sound: *heartbeat.*

Her fangs slid down before she even realized it, sharp and aching, catching the fluorescent glow. The noise of their emergence. a soft, wet click, made her flinch, but not enough to stop her body from moving.

She turned back toward the gurney. The patient lay half-conscious, his arm wrapped in gauze that was already darkening with blood. One more heartbeat. One more breath.

The scent filled her head like music.

Her body leaned forward before her mind caught up. She could *feel* the warmth radiating from his skin, the whisper of his pulse calling to her with every throb.

Her mouth parted.

Her breath trembled against his wrist.

Then…

No!

The word hit her like a slap, her own voice, buried deep but furious. She jerked back so violently she nearly toppled the tray beside her. Metal clattered across the floor.

Evelyn stumbled into the wall, pressing the back of her hand against her mouth. Her fangs ached, her jaw locked tight, and a low, guttural sound escaped her throat. A sound that wasn't human.

Her vision pulsed with red.

She tasted air, blood, storm, *him*.

He was closer now. She could feel him even before his shadow stretched across the floor toward her, calm and steady, his presence a counterpoint to her frenzy.

"You fight it too hard," his voice murmured.

Evelyn swallowed against the burn, shaking her head, every muscle straining not to turn toward him again.

"Stay away," she rasped, but even to her own ears it sounded like a plea.

The red emergency lights strobed again, catching on the wet sheen across her wrist. For a dizzying moment, it didn't look like blood at all; it looked like wine. Dark and sacred, shimmering with something more than life.

Her throat burned.

The sound of the patient's heartbeat still echoed in her mind and her own dead pulse tried to mimic it, rising with every breath she didn't need. The hunger she'd spent so much time burying stirred, stretching inside her like a waking animal.

You're not that anymore, she told herself. *You're careful. You're in control.*

But the scent laughed at her discipline.

She braced a hand on the wall, fingers curling against the cold tile as the generator hummed overhead. The storm outside deepened, thunder rolling through the bones of the hospital. Each vibration seemed to crawl under her skin, stirring something deeper, older.

Faint but unmistakable, that same resonant *hum* she'd felt earlier with Lucian was beneath it all. It threaded through the air like a calling tone, harmonizing with her hunger until she couldn't tell which belonged to her and which to him.

Her reflection in the glass cabinet caught her eye: pupils blown wide, lips parted. For a fraction of a second, her fangs glinted in the crimson light.

She slammed her eyes shut.

"Evelyn."

Her name was spoken softly, like an invocation.

She turned.

At the far end of the corridor stood Lucian Devereaux. Barefoot. Bare-chested. The bandages across his torso were soaked through, and the faint crest-shaped scar over his heart glowed like embers through the red haze.

The hum deepened, reverberating through her bones, through the blood drying on her skin.

Evelyn's hunger snapped tight; half terror, half desire.

"You shouldn't be awake," she managed, though her voice came out low and rough.

Lucian took a step closer, his eyes luminous even in the dim light. "Neither should you."

The scent of blood thickened between them.

Evelyn pressed her palms against the cold tile, trying to anchor herself in the sterile bite of reality. The blood's scent still clung to her, and each breath she didn't need made it worse.

Her fangs throbbed. Her heartbeat wasn't hers. It was the patient's, echoing inside her skull.

One taste, her instincts whispered. *One drop, and you'll be steady again.*

But another voice cut through, older and quieter. Her own, from a lifetime ago.

Never from the unwilling. Never again.

She saw it then, clear as if it were happening now: the alley behind a jazz bar a lifetime ago, the first time she'd woken hungry after her turning. The man she'd drained without meaning to, his terrified eyes still open as dawn broke. The vow that came after, spoken through tears and ash.

If I must live on blood, let it be from those who choose to give it.

That promise had been her anchor through what seemed like decades of restraint, of surviving quietly in the shadows between hospital corridors and midnight alleyways. Now the scent was burning through her resolve, unraveling every thread of that fragile discipline.

Her nails scraped against the tile. Her throat felt raw, her body trembling with the effort of denial.

"You can't fight hunger with shame," Lucian's voice murmured again, impossible to tell if it came from across the hall or from inside her head.

She shut her eyes tight. "You don't know me."

"I do," he said. "Because I've been where you are."

The hum of his aura pulsed faintly beneath the storm outside, like a second heartbeat aligning with her own. It soothed but also tempted.

Evelyn dug her teeth into her lower lip, tasting her own blood.

Never from the unwilling.

She repeated it again and again, like a prayer against the thunder.

With an agonizingly slow pace, the hunger began to recede. Not gone, but contained, coiled like a serpent just beneath her ribs.

Her knees shook with the effort of staying upright. Sweat, or what passed for it, beaded at her temple. The corridor's red light flickered again, and she realized Lucian's silhouette was closer now, his expression unreadable in the crimson haze.

The corridor emptied slowly, noise fading to the low hum of the generator and the far-off rhythm of rain. Evelyn moved on unsteady legs toward the restroom, each step mechanical, each breath a hollow imitation of calm.

She pushed open the door and let it close behind her. The fluorescent light above flickered once, then steadied into a dim, clinical glow. The air was thick with the smell of disinfectant and copper, the ghost of blood still clinging to her skin.

At the sink, she turned on the water and scrubbed hard, watching pink tendrils spiral down the drain. Her hands wouldn't stop shaking. The blood was gone, but the heat of it remained, seared into her senses.

When she finally looked up, her reflection didn't meet her halfway.

The woman in the mirror stood too still, her face pale as porcelain, her pupils dilated wide. For a heartbeat, she looked like herself again, tired and wary. Human enough to pass.

Then the lights flickered.

Her eyes burned crimson.

Not a trick of light. Not the faint red haze she'd fought to suppress over time. This was something deeper, unrestrained; a pure, feral gleam that split through her composure like a fracture in glass.

She stumbled back from the mirror, hand clamped over her mouth, but the reflection didn't flinch. It only stared unblinking and accusatory. As if something inside her had finally woken after too long asleep.

"No," she whispered. "Not again."

Her voice echoed in the tiled room, too thin to drown out the low hum that had haunted her since Lucian's arrival. It thrummed faintly through the walls, through her pulse, through the red glow behind her eyes.

She forced herself to look again.

The reflection stared back. It was crimson-eyed and sharp-toothed, Beautiful in the way disasters were beautiful just before they destroyed everything.

Evelyn pressed her palm to the cool glass, trembling.

If the hunger was this strong now, she thought, *what would happen when the next body came through those ER doors?*

The generator lights flickered once more, washing the mirror in red.

And this time, when the power steadied, the reflection didn't blink.

Chapter 5

Silent Recognition

The door to Lucian's recovery room clicked shut behind her, sealing out the hum of the ICU.

Only two lights remained: the soft green pulse of the heart monitor and the bruised glow of Crescent City bleeding through the half-open blinds. Neon signs shimmered across the linoleum floor: *bar blues, pharmacy red, motel gold.* Painting his still form in fractured colors.

Evelyn hesitated at the threshold.

The machines whispered, steady and deceptive. If she hadn't seen what he was and what *he* made her feel, she might have believed he was just another trauma patient. However, the shadows around him didn't move like ordinary darkness. They seemed to lean toward him, drawn by something unseen.

Outside, the storm had quieted. The city below steamed in its aftermath, rain-slick streets glowing like oil, the river beyond reflecting the fractured lights of the skyline. The entire world felt heavy and awake.

Lucian lay half-reclined against the pillows, the faint glow of the monitor tracing green light over his chest. His skin was too pale, even for one of her kind, and the faint crest-shaped scar over his heart pulsed in time with the machine's rhythm, as though mocking it.

Evelyn's reflection wavered faintly in the window beside him: a silhouette haloed in neon, her eyes catching just enough red to remind her that she wasn't safe. From herself or from him.

She stepped closer. The scent of antiseptic filled the air, but underneath it she caught something else, faint and electric. Not blood. *Power.*

"You shouldn't be awake," she said softly, the same words she'd spoken before, but they sounded different this time, more uncertain.

Lucian's eyes opened, silver-gray and unfocused, catching the neon light like a blade.

"Neither should you."

His voice was low, roughened by pain, memory, or both. She couldn't tell which. The heart monitor kept its calm, synthetic rhythm.

Evelyn lingered at the foot of his bed, torn between duty and something far more dangerous.

"You shouldn't be here," he murmured, eyes slipping toward her neck, toward the faint pulse that wasn't supposed to be there. "Not when you're starving."

Her jaw tightened. "You don't know anything about me."

He smiled faintly, not cruelly, but knowingly. "You think the city hides its hunger better than we do?"

Outside, thunder rolled again in the distance. Although softer now, like a promise rather than a threat.

Evelyn took another step forward, the green glow sliding over her face. The distance between them felt electric.

"Then tell me," she whispered, "what are you really doing here, Lucian Devereaux?"

His smile faded, replaced by something far older than weariness. "Trying to remember what we were before we forgot ourselves."

Lucian's gaze lingered on her for a heartbeat longer, the pulse on the monitor keeping steady time between them. Then his expression shifted. A flicker of confusion, of pain, before his breath hitched sharply.

The green line on the monitor stuttered.

"Lucian?" Evelyn's voice dropped, her instincts cutting through the haze of unease. She stepped forward, the cold professionalism of the nurse overtaking the wary distance she'd held a moment ago.

He tried to speak, but the words dissolved into a sound like wind through hollow glass. His body arched slightly, fingers clutching at the sheet, veins standing out pale and luminous under his skin. The faint crest over his heart blazed once with dull light and then dimmed.

The monitor's tone spiked, flatlined for a fraction of a second, then began to skip erratically.

"No, no, stay with me…" Evelyn reached the bedside, her hands already checking his pulse even though she knew it was useless. It wasn't a human rhythm she was trying to find.

For a moment, she felt it, a flicker beneath her palm, slow and unnatural, like something waking rather than dying.

Then nothing.

Lucian's head rolled to the side, lips parted slightly, eyes half-lidded but unfocused. Whatever strength he'd summoned before was gone. The air around him grew heavier, the faint hum that had always followed him fading like an extinguished current.

The heart monitor continued its uneven pulse, confused by what it was reading.

Evelyn's throat tightened. "Lucian?"

She leaned closer, scanning his face, his chest, the strange crest over his heart. The mark wasn't glowing anymore, but it hadn't disappeared either. The lines seemed to move subtly, like ink shifting under the skin, as if alive but dormant.

A faint chill touched the air, brushing over her arm. The light in the room dimmed, just slightly, as if something unseen had drawn breath.

Evelyn hesitated. Every instinct screamed to call for help, but a deeper instinct told her this wasn't something anyone else should see.

"Don't do this," she whispered, though she wasn't sure if she was speaking to him or to the quiet, ancient part of herself that recognized the stillness before change.

She reached out again, fingertips brushing his collarbone. His skin was cold. Too cold.

Outside, lightning cracked, illuminating the skyline. For an instant, the reflection in the window showed both of them. Her face and eyes faintly red in the neon light, and his lying still beside her.

Then the lights flickered. The heart monitor stuttered again.

And Lucian Devereaux didn't move.

The heart monitor gave a sudden, uncertain chirp.

Evelyn froze, her hand still resting against his chest. Beneath her fingertips, something shifted; a tremor, faint but deliberate, like the first ripple of a tide returning to shore.

Then his pulse surged once, twice.

Lucian's eyes snapped open.

They were no longer just silver. Darkness threaded through the irises like smoke in mercury, twisting and coiling until both colors seemed to move within each other. It wasn't human, not even by her standards. His gaze locked onto hers with frightening precision, as though he'd been waiting in that half-death for her to be close enough.

Evelyn's breath caught. The room fell away. There was only the faint sound that had followed her since the trauma bay now resonating louder and deeper, until she could feel it thrumming against her ribs.

"Lucian…"

He moved before she finished, his hand shooting up to grip her wrist. His touch was cold, but not lifeless, more like stone under moonlight. The crest over his heart flared once, a faint pulse of light bleeding through the bandage.

"You… *remember*," he rasped, voice raw, words dragging like something pulled from a long sleep.

Evelyn leaned closer despite herself, caught between dread and recognition. "What are you talking about?"

His grip tightened; not painfully, but enough that she couldn't pull away. His eyes darkened further, the black bleeding into silver until they looked like eclipsed moons.

"It's starting again," he whispered. "The circle… it's breaking."

The heart monitor shrieked, the sound slicing through the silence. Evelyn turned toward it instinctively, and when she looked back, his hand had fallen away.

Lucian's eyes fluttered shut. The sound receded like a tide going out, leaving her breathless and hollow in its wake.

The monitor steadied again. One pulse. Then another.

He was alive. Or at least something close to it.

Evelyn stood there in the half-dark, her hand still tingling where he'd touched her, the city's neon light crawling across his still form.

And she realized, with a cold certainty that settled deep in her bones, that whatever had just stirred inside Lucian Devereaux had also awakened something inside her. Something she'd spent too much pretending no longer existed.

The room was silent again, but the stillness wasn't empty.

Evelyn's pulse throbbed faintly in her throat. Then another rhythm joined it, steady and patient, as a second heartbeat layered beneath her own. The sound wasn't coming from inside her, though. It came from *him.*

Lucian.

Even unconscious, his presence filled the room like a gravitational field. She could *feel* him, something in his blood, in whatever current ran through his veins instead of life, syncing with hers.

It wasn't pain. It wasn't even hunger. It was magnetic.

Each beat of her heart matched his, the two rhythms aligning until they were indistinguishable. Her breath hitched, her body leaning slightly closer without meaning to, as if her blood itself was being tugged toward him.

The faint glow from the crest over his heart pulsed once, and the sound deepened. The machines around them seemed to fade to a dull murmur, the air thickening until she could hear something *beneath* the hum.

A voice.

Soft. Low. Whispering a pattern of syllables that didn't belong to any language she knew. It was old; older than cities, older than her kind. The words rolled like the ocean against stone, familiar in a way that made her bones ache.

She staggered a half-step back, pressing a hand to her temple.

The whisper grew louder; not in her ears, but in her *mind*. A single phrase rose above the rest, syllables curling through her thoughts like smoke.

"Aelthra ven'nai…"

The sound sent a chill down her spine. Her reflection in the window caught the faintest glimmer of red in her eyes again, pulsing in perfect time with his heart monitor.

"Lucian," she breathed, though he didn't stir. "What are you doing to me?"

The hum ceased abruptly. The pull snapped, leaving her gasping, unsteady, her body aching from the sudden emptiness.

She stumbled back against the counter, gripping it hard. Her pulse was her own again, but the echo of his rhythm lingered in her blood, like the echo of a song she almost remembered.

Then, from the bed, Lucian exhaled a long, deliberate breath. The crest over his heart dimmed, fading back to stillness.

Evelyn pressed a trembling hand to her sternum. The beat there was no longer her own rhythm. it was theirs.

And in the silence that followed, she realized she could still *feel* him. Even with his eyes closed, even as machines whirled their sterile lullaby, something inside him called to her still.

Something ancient. Something waiting.

The monitors hummed softly in the dark, their steady pulse the only sound breaking the hush. Evelyn stood frozen, her hand still pressed to her chest, when a faint light flickered in the corner of her vision.

Lucian stirred.

The crest over his heart; once dim, once sleeping, flared to life again. But this time, it wasn't the elegant sigil she'd glimpsed before. It shifted, reformed, alive beneath the skin. A new pattern emerged, coiling outward from the original mark: a spiral wrapped in fine, jagged lines like *thorns made of light.*

Evelyn's breath caught. The glow was faint, not bright enough to illuminate the room, but it pulsed with purpose, like a heartbeat that wasn't his alone.

Then her wrist burned.

A shock of warmth lanced up her arm, sharp enough to make her gasp. She looked down, half-expecting blood but what she saw stole the air from her lungs.

There, beneath the skin on the inside of her wrist, the same sigil shimmered faintly to life. A spiral, delicate and mirrored to his, its edges pricking outward like the thorns of a rose. The mark pulsed once, perfectly in sync with the one glowing on Lucian's chest.

For a single, unbearable heartbeat, the room seemed to stop breathing.

Her pulse, his pulse, the monitor, all one rhythm.

The symbols glowed brighter, the air around them vibrating with a low hum that made the metal IV stand tremble. The scent of ozone filled the air again, sharp and clean, mingling with antiseptic and storm.

Then, just as suddenly, it faded.

The light on Lucian's chest sank back into stillness. The mark on Evelyn's wrist dimmed until it was nothing but ordinary skin, smooth and unbroken, as if it had never been there. But the warmth lingered, a faint ache that pulsed with every beat of her heart.

She staggered back a step, clutching her wrist. "What the hell was that…?"

Lucian didn't answer. He lay perfectly still, his breathing even, his face calm and almost serene.

Evelyn's reflection in the window caught her eye again, and this time she saw the faintest shimmer of the sigil's outline ghosting across her skin before vanishing entirely.

Whatever had happened, it wasn't just a coincidence. It wasn't just hunger or hallucination.

They were connected now. Bound by something older than blood.

And deep in her bones, Evelyn knew: the mark wasn't a warning. It was a summons.

The last trace of light faded from their skin, swallowed by the dim red wash of the heart monitor's glow.

Evelyn stood motionless, her pulse still tangled with a rhythm that wasn't hers.

Outside the window, lightning spidered across the clouds and for an instant its reflection split her image in two: the woman she'd spent so much time pretending to be, and the creature who could never quite forget what she was.

She stared at Lucian. He looked almost peaceful now, though his stillness wasn't human rest. His features seemed carved from moonlight and shadow. Even unconscious, he radiated something magnetic, ancient, and heartbreakingly familiar.

Evelyn's fingers brushed her wrist again, searching for the sigil that had burned there moments ago. Nothing. Only a ghost of warmth, and beneath it, a promise she couldn't name.

You remember.

The words he'd spoken before echoed through her mind. Remember what? A life before this one? A curse looping through centuries?

Her logical mind, what remained of it after so much restraint and hiding, whispered to walk away. To call security, hand him over, and bury whatever had just happened under routine and fluorescent light.

But the other part of her, the part that had woken the moment his eyes met hers, couldn't move.

The whisper from earlier; those ancient syllables she didn't understand stirred faintly again, like the echo of a vow spoken long ago. Though she didn't know the language, she understood the intent.

It wasn't warning her to run. It was binding her closer.

Evelyn reached out, almost against her will, and adjusted the blanket over his chest. Her hand lingered just above his heart, feeling the faint rhythm that still pulsed beneath the skin.

Something deep within her, a hunger, a memory, a longing, answered in kind.

She should have been terrified. Instead, she felt a strange calm, fragile as spun glass. Whatever had tied them together tonight was older than fear. Older, perhaps, than choice.

Evelyn exhaled, steadying herself as thunder rolled in from the sea.

She didn't know who Lucian Devereaux truly was. She didn't know what the sigil meant.

However, as she stood watching over him, her reflection wreathed in stormlight, one truth crystallized in her chest:

Whatever fate had marked them with, it had chosen her as his guardian, whether she wanted it or not.

And though she trembled, she couldn't deny it. She didn't want to run. She wanted to protect him.

Even if doing so meant losing herself.

Chapter 6

A Warning in the Alley

The double doors of St. Augustine's whispered shut behind Evelyn, sealing off the antiseptic brightness of the hospital for the soft, pulsing dark outside.

Midnight rain had left the city glistening. Mist curled off the wet cobblestones of the rear alley, weaving through trash bins and the faint steam rising from nearby storm drains. The sodium lights overhead flickered in uneven intervals; orange, then dark, then orange again. This effect casting the brick walls in shifting, uneasy color.

Evelyn tugged her scrubs jacket tighter, though she didn't feel the chill the way she used to. The humid Crescent City air was heavy with magnolia and diesel, but beneath it lingered something else, ozone from the distant storm rolling in over the gulf, that same restless charge that seemed to have followed her ever since Lucian arrived.

She exhaled slowly, watching the mist coil around her breath. Every nerve in her body still hummed with the aftershock of what had happened earlier. The things that raged the conflict inside of her; *the mark,* the shared pulse, the whisper that wasn't quite a dream.

She'd washed her wrist raw in the staff sink before leaving, but she swore she could still feel the sigil's warmth there, ghosting beneath her skin like a faint ember that refused to die.

The alley stretched out ahead of her, quiet except for the distant buzz of a transformer and the low hiss of rain against the pavement. Somewhere deeper in the city, a siren rose and fell, swallowed by the fog.

Evelyn slung her bag over her shoulder and started down the narrow lane toward the staff parking lot. Her shoes clicked softly against the stones, each step echoing just a little too loudly in the stillness.

The storm's first low rumble reached her then, rolling through the alley like the growl of something ancient waking from sleep.

She paused, glancing over her shoulder.

For a moment, she thought she saw movement, a shadow separating itself from the deeper dark at the far end of the alley.

But when the light flickered again, it was gone.

Evelyn took another step, then stopped.

That feeling pulled taut in her chest. A prickle at the back of her neck, the unmistakable awareness of being watched.

The mist seemed thicker now, moving with purpose instead of drifting. It coiled around her ankles, sliding across the slick stones like breath. The hum of the sodium lights faltered again, throwing the alley into half-dark.

She turned her head slightly, not enough to look behind her, just enough to listen.

At first, nothing. Only the rain. The hiss of water sliding from a fire escape.

Then it came softly. Barely audible. A footstep.

Not the echo of her own. A fraction behind her rhythm. Someone matching her pace.

Her pulse quickened despite herself. She'd heard footsteps like that before, when the hunters still stalked the back streets of Baton Rouge. The memory came unbidden: the smell of silver, the sound of ash sizzling where it shouldn't.

Her senses sharpened automatically. The world around her narrowed into scent, sound, movement. The faint tang of rust; something else, something deliberate.

She shifted her bag from one shoulder to the other, letting her right hand drop casually toward the hem of her jacket, where a slim glass vial rested in her pocket;

synthetic blood mixed with a paralytic. A precaution she hadn't ever used.

Another step behind her. Closer this time.

Evelyn's throat tightened, fangs pressing faintly against her lips. Not from hunger, but instinct. The predator beneath her skin stirred awake, tasting the air for danger.

She reached the corner of the alley where the old brick met a narrow side passage choked with vines and shadows. The path led back toward the hospital's loading bay, a dead end. She hesitated, calculating.

Another sound, which sounded like fabric brushing against wet brick. Someone was definitely there.

She turned her head slightly, catching only a shape, a darker shadow among the fog. Broad-shouldered and moving with purpose.

The scent reached her next: leather, damp air, and beneath it a faint trace of something she hadn't smelled in years.

Silver.

Her pulse stuttered.

Whoever followed her wasn't just curious. They were dangerous. And they knew what she was.

Evelyn quickened her pace, the hospital's rear parking lot finally coming into view through the thinning mist. Rows of empty cars gleamed wet beneath the flickering streetlights, the puddles between them reflecting fractured bands of orange and gray.

She'd almost reached her own car when a shadow detached itself from the darkness at the edge of the lot.

The figure slowly and deliberately stepped into the sodium glow.

He was tall, lean but solid, dressed in a weathered leather coat that hung just past his knees. Rain clung to the dark strands of his hair, slicking them back from a face carved in sharp planes. He was handsome in a way that looked both rough and old, like stone worn by wind.

The smell hit her before he spoke: leather, woodsmoke, and beneath it, the unmistakable tang of *silver*. It prickled along her nerves like static.

She froze, instincts warring between confrontation and retreat. He didn't move closer but his presence filled the space between them like a closing door.

His eyes caught the light for just a second; gray, but with something unnatural behind them. Predatory recognition.

Not human. But not quite vampire, either.

Evelyn's voice came out lower than she meant it to, steadier too. "You followed me from the ER."

He tilted his head slightly, the motion calm, assessing. "Hard place to talk in there," he said, his voice roughened by smoke or age, or maybe both.

She took a measured step backward, her heel brushing a puddle. "If you're looking for blood, find another donor."

That earned her a faint smile, humorless and knowing. "Not what I came for."

Lightning flared somewhere beyond the city skyline, reflecting in his eyes like silver fire.

For a moment, neither of them moved. The storm growled low in the distance, and the scent of magnolia drifted between them, faint but persistent, mingling with the edge of rain.

Then he took a slow step forward, boots scraping wet stone.

The faint glint of metal at his belt caught her attention. Stakes, slender and dulled from use.

Hunter.

Or worse, something that hunted both kinds.

He stopped a few paces from her, close enough that the air between them thickened with the scent of rain and silver.

For a heartbeat, neither spoke. The only sound was the steady patter of droplets dripping from the eaves and the low hum of the storm closing in over Crescent City.

Then, his gaze sharpened. The faint amusement in it vanished, replaced by something colder, almost regretful.

"Royal blood draws death," he said, voice low and gravel-edged. "Stay clear of the prince if you value your unbeating heart."

The words cut through the rain like a blade.

Evelyn's stomach twisted. "The prince?" she repeated softly, but he didn't move, didn't blink. His expression didn't even shift, though the muscles in his jaw flexed once, tight.

Lightning split the sky above the hospital, flashing white across the wet cobblestones. For an instant, the light caught the faintest trace of scars at his throat.

They were burn marks; circular, like old silver wounds.

He wasn't bluffing.

Whoever he was, he'd fought creatures like her and survived.

The storm vividly stirred, blowing a strand of hair across her face as the mist eddied around them. She could feel the truth in his words like static under her skin, vibrating against the faint mark still hidden on her wrist.

Royal blood. Prince.

Lucian.

But before she could speak, the stranger shifted his weight subtly. Just enough to remind her that he could vanish as easily as he'd appeared.

Evelyn's pulse quickened, though her expression stayed carefully still. The rain was coming down harder now, a steady rhythm against the asphalt, the drops sliding down her hair and collar.

She took a step forward, closing the space between them by a fraction. "What did you just say?" Her voice was low but edged with steel. "Who are you calling *the prince?*"

The man didn't flinch, but his eyes flicked briefly to her wrist where the sigil had burned hours earlier, invisible now but still tingling beneath her skin. The look was deliberate. Knowing.

"You already know," he murmured.

A muscle jumped in her jaw. "If you think you can just follow me and throw riddles at me, you're wasting your time." She took another step. The air between them buzzed faintly, her instincts rising to the surface, fangs pressing lightly against her lower lip. "What do you want from me?"

He gave a dry, humorless laugh. "Want? Nothing. You've already given enough just by standing too close to him."

Evelyn frowned, confusion cutting through the fear. "Lucian? You mean *him*, don't you?"

The stranger's gaze hardened at the name, the rain catching in the stubble on his face. "Don't say it out loud. Names have weight. And his carries an old curse."

Lightning cracked overhead again, followed by the heavy roll of thunder that rattled the nearby dumpsters. Evelyn stood her ground, refusing to let the tremor in her hands show.

"You know what he is," she pressed. "Tell me."

He regarded her for a long, unreadable moment, the mist swirling between them. There was something ancient in his eyes now. It might have been weariness or maybe even pity.

"He's not what you think," the man said finally. "And if you were smart, you'd let him die before the rest of us do."

Her stomach twisted. "What the hell does that mean?"

He didn't answer.

The sodium light flickered again, throwing his shadow long across the pavement.

Evelyn stepped forward. One more question forming on her lips…

The light above them sputtered once, dimmed, then flared again. Long enough for her to see the faintest curl of a smirk at the corner of his mouth.

"You ask too many questions for someone who's survived this long," he said, his tone not cruel, but almost… respectful.

Before she could reply, the shadows behind him seemed to deepen. The mist rolled in thick and low, rising like smoke. One blink, and he was gone. His shape dissolving into the darkness as if it had swallowed him whole.

Evelyn spun, scanning the alley, but there was nothing. No footsteps. No sound but the rain hissing against the concrete.

Only the air itself felt heavier now. It was charged with static and the faint metallic tang that burned at the edge of her senses.

She inhaled sharply. Silver.

The scent clung to the space he'd just occupied, bitter and sharp, coating the back of her throat. It mixed with the rain, the mist, the faint sweetness of magnolia drifting in from the street beyond.

Her pulse quickened. She knew that smell too well. Silver meant hunters. Silver meant death.

The puddles shimmered under the flickering lights, ripples spreading where nothing had moved. Evelyn turned a slow circle, her eyes adjusting to the gloom, but the alley was empty.

No trace of him. No sound of retreating boots. Only the metallic aftertaste of a warning she couldn't ignore.

The thunder rolled again, closer this time, echoing off the brick walls. Evelyn's reflection in a car window caught her eye, wet hair clinging to her cheek, eyes burning faintly red in the sodium glow.

She realized she was trembling, not from fear, but from the strange, furious certainty that none of this was a coincidence.

The rain softened, tapering into a thin mist that clung to her skin. The air still tasted of silver, but beneath it was something else; her own resolve, cooling and hardening like tempered glass.

Evelyn stood there in the half-light, staring at the spot where the stranger had vanished. His words echoed in her head, each syllable pressing into her like a brand:

Royal blood draws death. Stay clear of the prince.

She could almost laugh. As if she'd ever been good at staying clear of danger.

Fear still coiled in her chest, a living thing, but it no longer dictated her movement. Instead, it fueled the steady burn rising in her veins. The same quiet defiance that had kept her alive all this time. Hunters, ancient bloodlines, prophecies; none of it changed what she'd seen in Lucian's eyes, or the pull that had tied their fates together the moment he'd whispered those first impossible words.

The mark on her wrist throbbed once, faint but insistent, like a heartbeat answering another from far away.

Evelyn lifted her chin toward the darkened sky, rain catching in her lashes, and whispered to no one, "Then let them come."

She turned toward the hospital lights, the mist swirling at her heels, her decision already made.

Whatever Lucian Devereaux was, he wasn't facing this alone.

Not while she still drew breath.

Chapter 7

Feeding in the Dark

The power failed just after midnight.

The hum of machines, the steady throb of fluorescent lights all blinked out at once, leaving the hospital wrapped in a silence so complete it felt physical. For one long heartbeat, St. Augustine's held its breath. Then the generators kicked in.

A dim red glow washed through the corridors, painting the walls in blood and shadow. The emergency lights pulsed unevenly, casting long, skeletal silhouettes that stretched and contracted with every flicker.

Evelyn moved through the shuttered east wing, her footsteps muffled on the linoleum. The air was warmer here. It was stale and faintly metallic. A forgotten part of the hospital. No patients. No staff. Just the distant hum of the backup power grid and the slow drip of condensation from the ceiling vents.

Outside, the blackout had spread through the city; she could hear it in the absence of noise. No traffic. No streetlights. Just the low rumble of thunder rolling across Crescent Bay and the faint hiss of rain against the old windows.

She paused at the corner where two corridors met, the red light from the emergency strips sliding over her face like a pulse. The smell of antiseptic lingered in the air, sharp enough to sting, but underneath it was something else, something fainter and seductive.

Blood.

It wasn't fresh, not yet. Just a trace threading through the air like a promise.

Her throat tightened. The hunger that had been coiling in her for nights now stirred fully awake, stretching in her chest like a restless animal.

She swallowed hard, forcing her breathing to stay even. The last of her "safe" feedings had been three nights ago, a stored donation from the blood bank, cold and lifeless. It had done little more than dull the ache.

Now, in the silence and dark, every trace of human scent was amplified. Every heartbeat on the floors above sounded too loud, too close.

She pressed her back to the wall and closed her eyes. The red light pulsed again, washing the world in a heartbeat's rhythm.

And with each throb, the metallic scent grew stronger.

It was coming from somewhere deeper in the wing, down past the storage rooms and shuttered operating suites.

Something was bleeding.

And Evelyn could feel it calling her.

Evelyn moved deeper into the darkened wing, her shoes whispering against the floor. The hospital seemed to exhale around her, the crackle of fluorescent bulbs trying to wake but failing.

The scent guided her like a thread through a labyrinth. Past the linen closet. Past the decommissioned nurses' station, where clipboards still hung on hooks, yellowed charts left behind years ago. The air grew thicker and sweeter, the copper tang of blood rising above the antiseptic veil.

Her pulse quickened in her throat. It shouldn't have, but the hunger had a way of tricking her body into remembering.

At the end of the corridor, a door stood slightly ajar. The faded lettering read "Phlebotomy – Restricted Access." A faint crimson glow leaked through the crack, painting the floor in a thin, trembling line.

Evelyn pushed it open.

Inside, the air was cooler, heavy with the sterile chill of refrigerated storage. A cart sat in the center of the room, an open tray of blood samples half-sorted beside an unplugged centrifuge. One of the storage units had failed when the blackout rolled through; the door hung ajar, condensation running down its metal face like sweat.

And there beneath the hum of emergency lights she could hear it: the slow, liquid heartbeat of stored blood.

The plastic bags, warm from the rising temperature, exhaled faint traces of iron and life.

Evelyn's fangs pressed against her lower lip.

Just a sip, she told herself. *Just enough to quiet the ache.*

Her hand trembled as she reached for one of the bags. The seal was cold and slick under her fingers.

She glanced toward the door and the empty hallway. There were no footsteps or witnesses.

The hunger pulsed again, urging her forward.

She lifted the blood bag to her lips.

And then…

A sound.

Low, pained. Human.

From somewhere beyond the phlebotomy room.

Evelyn froze.

The sound had been soft, barely more than a breath. A muffled groan, maybe, or the drag of something heavy across tile. It could have come from the corridor… or from the shadows pooling in the far corner of the room.

She held perfectly still, listening.

The generator's distant rumble filled the silence, a steady mechanical heartbeat. The emergency lights flickered, throwing the room into shifting halves of light and dark. Every time the red glow returned, it warped the edges of her reflection in the chrome cabinets, showing her face hollowed with eyes rimmed in shadow.

Another noise. Fainter this time. A scrape, then nothing.

Her senses stretched outward, instinct sharpened by hunger. She tasted air like a predator: ozone, alcohol, copper, and beneath it something faintly human, but fading fast.

"Hello?" she whispered before catching herself. Her voice sounded strange. It was too low, too resonant.

Silence answered.

She scanned the rows of counters, the empty gurney, the open refrigerator door leaking a slow trickle of condensation onto the tile. Nothing moved. No breath but her own. No heartbeat within the room's radius.

Her jaw ached. The muscles along her neck quivered with restraint.

If there had been someone here, they would have been gone by now. Or she was imagining things; hallucinations born of deprivation.

She turned back toward the tray of blood bags. The light caught the translucent red inside, glimmering like rubies suspended in plastic. Her hunger clawed at her control.

Evelyn exhaled, slow and deliberate. Then she sank onto the stool beside the cart and lifted the bag again.

Her fangs brushed the edge of the plastic, a shiver racing through her spine as the faintest whiff of blood met the air.

Just a sip, she thought again, closing her eyes.

The red light pulsed once more.

And somewhere, beyond the walls of the shuttered wing, thunder rolled closer.

The blood bag slipped from her hand.

It wasn't the thunder this time. The sound that jolted her came from the corridor. A body hitting the floor. Hard.

Evelyn was on her feet before she thought to move, the stool rolling backward and clattering against the wall. She pushed open the phlebotomy door and stepped into the hallway, red light flashing across her face in uneven waves.

A man staggered toward her from the far end of the corridor. His outline wavered in the gloom. He had broad shoulders, a torn denim jacket soaked through with rain, and something darker. He took two uneven steps, then crumpled against the wall, smearing a crimson streak down the tile before collapsing.

"Hey! Hey! Don't move," Evelyn said, rushing to him. Her voice went into instinctive nurse mode, steady and practiced even as her pulse flared in her throat.

The man was young. He was in his mid-twenties, maybe. Skin ghost-pale beneath the grime, eyes half-lidded. His shirt was shredded at the abdomen where the knife wound gaped, dark blood bubbling sluggishly with every shallow breath.

"Stab wound," she murmured, already pulling the torn fabric aside. "No compression bandage. God…"

She tore open a cabinet, found a gauze pack, and pressed it hard against the wound. The warmth flooded her hands instantly.

The scent hit her like a wave.

She gritted her teeth, forcing herself to keep her grip steady.

"Stay with me," she said, leaning close. "You hear me? Stay with me."

His eyes fluttered, unfocused. He mumbled something. Broken syllables, maybe a name, but the words dissolved into a wet cough.

She glanced down. The blood was pooling too fast. Too much. She could feel his heartbeat fluttering beneath her palms like a trapped bird.

"No, no, no…" Evelyn's voice broke. "Come on, don't do this now."

She worked automatically; pressure, airway check, searching for a pulse that faltered more each second. Her training took over, hands moving even as her mind reeled.

Then she realized there was no time. No human treatment could stop the bleeding now.

His body shuddered once, breath catching, and Evelyn froze. The metallic scent of his blood filled the corridor, bright and terrible.

She felt the monster inside her stir.

But she held her ground, trembling.

Evelyn's breath came in shallow bursts. Her hands, slick with blood, pressed uselessly against the wound that would not close. The man's pulse fluttered weakly beneath her fingers; there, then gone, then faint again.

He's dying.

Her human mind said it with clinical certainty. Her nurse's training tallied the facts: massive blood loss, punctured lung, likely hypovolemic shock. There was no saving him without surgery or transfusion. Time he didn't have.

But beneath that calm assessment, something ancient and cold whispered another truth:
He doesn't have to die.

Her throat burned. The copper scent coiled into her lungs, sweet and sharp, cutting through the air. She could almost *taste* it already, the iron tang blooming at the back of her tongue.

"No," she hissed under her breath, shaking her head as if to clear it. "No, no, I'm not doing this!"

The words sounded thin in the empty corridor, swallowed by the red pulse of emergency lights.

Her fangs ached, pressing against her gums, begging for release.

She clamped her jaw shut until she felt enamel creak. Her phantom pulse throbbed in her ears.

The man moaned softly, blood bubbling at the edge of his lips. His gaze caught hers for a second; clouded, desperate, still trying to live.

And something inside her *snapped.*

She wanted to help him. She *needed* to help him.

But part of her, the darker, buried part, was already imagining the heat of his blood against her tongue, the way it would flood her senses, the relief that would follow.

Her hands trembled. Her body leaned forward, unbidden, every muscle tuned to that siren scent.

He's dying anyway, the whisper urged. *Let it mean something.*

Evelyn's vision blurred at the edges. The ghost of her heartbeat synchronized with his fading one, a dissonant echo.

Her breath hitched. Her pupils widened, catching the red glow like twin shards of glass.

She hovered there, torn between duty and hunger, healer and predator. Her whole body was straining against the inevitable pull.

Evelyn's resistance fractured like thin glass under pressure.

The man's pulse faltered again; one fragile beat, then another, weaker. His blood seeped between her fingers, hot and slick, carrying the last of his life.

She didn't think. She *moved.*

Her hands shifted from compressing the wound to cradling him, lifting his head gently from the cold tile. He groaned in a wet and broken sound. She met his eyes.

"Shh," she whispered, voice trembling but soft. "It's all right… just breathe."

Her pupils dilated fully, the faint crimson gleam deepening until her gaze caught his like a snare. His panic slackened, eyelids fluttering. The thrall unfurled between them, invisible but absolute, wrapping around his fading consciousness like silk.

She leaned closer.

Her breath brushed the torn flesh at his side. The scent was unbearable now, sharp and alive, pulling every thought into its orbit.

"Just breathe," she murmured again, and then she lowered her mouth to the wound.

Her fangs pierced his torn skin with an effortless, instinctive motion.

Heat flooded her senses.

The taste was electric, burning through the hollow ache in her chest and blooming into something like ecstasy. Her hunger roared awake, every nerve alive with the pulse of his blood as it filled her mouth.

The man's body jerked once in her arms, then relaxed. His breathing steadied under the thrall, the fear dissolving into a hazy calm. She could feel his heartbeat syncing with her own unnatural rhythm, a slow echo that resonated through her bones.

For a moment, there was nothing but the rhythm and the taste. The world outside that fragile heartbeat ceased to exist. There was no storm, no flickering lights and no vow whispered to an empty sky a long time ago.

Only warmth. Only silence. Only *hunger*.

She drew back slightly, lips slick, breath unsteady. The wound still bled faintly beneath her hand, the man's pulse flickering against her palm.

He was still alive. Barely.

And she felt *awake* in a way she hadn't in years.

The man's breath hitched.

Evelyn froze, her senses still reeling from the rush of borrowed life. The heartbeat beneath her hand fluttered, then steadied, faint but undeniable.

He was breathing again.

His eyelids fluttered, the dull glaze of near-death clearing to reveal eyes gone glassy with confusion. His pupils were wide, unfocused, the residue of her thrall still holding him in its hazy grip.

"Easy," Evelyn murmured, her voice raw. "Don't move. You're safe."

She wasn't sure if she meant him or herself.

The scent of blood still clung to the air. It coated her tongue, her lips, her thoughts. But the hunger had dulled now, replaced by something else: a hollow, trembling awareness.

She looked down at him. Color had begun to return to his face, faint but visible. The jagged edges of the wound no longer pulsed with that frantic leak of life; instead, they seemed… muted. Slowed.

It wasn't healing; humans didn't heal that fast. But the bleeding had ceased enough to keep him alive.

Evelyn pressed her hand over the wound again, her own fingers shaking. She could feel the echo of his heartbeat still resonating faintly through her veins.

He groaned softly, trying to speak. "Wha… what happened?"

She leaned close, brushing his hair from his forehead, her voice low and steady. "You were hurt. You lost a lot of blood. I stopped it."

That was partly true.

His gaze drifted toward her, hazy and uncomprehending, and for a terrible moment she thought he might *see* the faint red in her eyes, the tremor of guilt that vibrated through her.

But then his head fell back against the tile, breath steadying, consciousness slipping again into fragile sleep.

Evelyn sat back on her heels, staring at her stained and trembling hands, not entirely her own.

The taste lingered on her tongue, sweet and damning.

And beneath the dull hum of the generator, she could hear it: the man's heart, still beating. Alive.

Because of her. And *because of what she'd done.*

Evelyn stayed crouched beside him long after his breathing settled into the shallow rhythm of sleep. The corridor was silent except for the distant hum of the generator and the faint drip of rain against the boarded windows.

Her hands still trembled. The scent of blood clung to her skin, soaked into her pulse. She stared down at the man she'd saved and fed from, something inside her twisted.

You swore you'd never do this.

She pressed the heel of her palm to her mouth, trying to block the taste, but it lingered. It wasn't just the memory of it, it was the *afterglow*. Her senses were alive, sharper than they'd ever been. The thrum of the hospital's backup grid vibrated through the walls. She could hear the faint rhythm of machinery two floors above, the steady drip of an IV line in some distant room.

Even stranger, the air seemed charged. When she looked at the man again, her vision shimmered. For the briefest instant, she saw something beyond him. Fragments. A street corner bathed in neon light. A flash of fear. A woman's voice calling his name.

Then it was gone.

Evelyn recoiled, breath catching in her throat.

The new awareness pulsed like static under her skin. Every heartbeat in the building felt distinct, like threads on a web she could almost touch. She clutched her chest, half expecting to feel her own heart racing. Of course, it was still. Cold. Unchanged.

Only her hunger had changed.

She looked at the unconscious man again, guilt tightening her jaw. She had saved his life, yes. However, she had crossed the line she'd drawn in blood and silence so long ago.

And the worst part was how *natural* it had felt.

The rush, the power, the instinct; it had all come back as if it had never left.

Evelyn rose slowly, wiping her hands on her scrubs, though the stains would never truly come out. The red emergency lights flickered once more, washing her reflection in the glass panel of the door. A face she barely recognized. Eyes faintly glowing. Fangs still half-bared.

She turned away before the lights dimmed again, her pulse ringing with echoes that didn't belong to her.

She was supposed to be a healer. But tonight had proven what she truly was… and what she was still becoming.

Chapter 8

The Prince's Truth

The storm had broken by the time Evelyn reached Lucian's recovery suite.

Rain still streaked the tall arched windows, tracing silver veins across the glass, but beyond them the city glowed faintly with wet streets reflecting the fractured light of gas lamps and neon signs. Crescent City looked half-drowned and half reborn while being wrapped in the lingering hush that always followed a tempest.

Inside, the room was quiet.

The machines that had once screamed alarms now murmured with their lights blinking in a steady rhythm with Lucian's pulse. The sterile brightness of hospital fluorescents had long since dimmed, replaced by a single standing lamp and the faint blue glow of the skyline. Shadows clung to the corners, moving when the rain shifted across the windows.

Lucian lay against the raised back of the hospital bed, pale as marble beneath the tangled sheets. He looked better than he had that night in the trauma bay. He was stronger and more composed, but there was still something otherworldly in the stillness of him.

Evelyn paused at the doorway, her hand brushing the frame. She had expected to feel fear or guilt or something resembling both, but instead, there was a quiet pull in her chest. It was a magnetic tension that drew her toward him despite every reason to stay away.

The scent of the sterile air lingered in the room, faint and sharp from the storm. It mingled with something darker, something like iron and smoke that seemed to belong to Lucian himself.

He stirred slightly, the motion slow, deliberate. When his eyes opened, they were a pale, impossible silver that caught the dim light like metal.

Evelyn took a step forward, her voice low. "Couldn't sleep?"

Lucian's lips curved faintly, almost human, almost not. "Sleep is… rare for my kind."

The rain whispered against the glass, soft and ceaseless, as the two of them regarded each other across the flickering shadows of the room.

Evelyn stepped closer, drawn by both duty and something less definable. The change in him was unmistakable.

The ashen pallor that had clung to Lucian when he'd first been brought in had softened to something more alive. Though "alive" didn't quite fit him. His skin still held that faint, unnatural luminescence that spoke of old blood and older magic, but there was color now, a subtle undertone of warmth threading through the ivory.

Even the monitors seemed to acknowledge the difference. His vitals that were once erratic now pulsed in a strange but steady rhythm. Not entirely human, no, but consistent. Controlled.

Evelyn's gaze flicked to the IV line that hung near his bed. The fluids had gone untouched for hours. His chart, still clipped to the stand, noted accelerated tissue recovery and near-complete stabilization of internal injuries. Every mortal physician who'd reviewed his case had shrugged in confusion. Evelyn knew better.

She could *feel* it.

The aura she had sensed that first night, the low, resonant hum, was stronger now, vibrating just beneath the skin of the air. It wasn't sound exactly, but something her bones recognized before her mind did.

Lucian sat up slightly, ignoring the pull of healing tissue, his movements fluid and precise. There was no wince, no hesitation, just a deliberate grace that made the hospital bed seem like an ill fit for him.

"You're healing faster than expected," Evelyn said softly, scanning his chart without really seeing it.

Lucian's gaze flicked to her, cool and knowing. "My kind tends to defy mortal expectations."

Lightning flared faintly in the distance, its reflection cutting through the rain-slick glass. For a heartbeat, the room was filled with silver light, and in it, Lucian looked almost regal. Not a patient, but a creature misplaced among men.

Evelyn looked away first. "You should still rest," she murmured, forcing her tone into something clinical.

A faint smile touched his lips. "Rest is for those who fear waking."

The words lingered, strange and heavy, as footsteps approached from the hallway. It was the quiet tread of the night-shift nurse coming to check the monitors.

Lucian's expression shifted, a shadow of intent passing through his eyes.

The door opened with a soft creak, and the night-shift nurse stepped inside. He was a tired-looking man in blue scrubs, balancing a clipboard and a mug of stale coffee. His gaze swept from the machines to Lucian, then to Evelyn, relief flickering over his face when he saw the monitors stable.

"Looks like our mystery patient's made a full turnaround," the nurse said, jotting a note on the chart. "Dr. Rollins'll be thrilled. Maybe he can stop muttering about medical miracles for five minutes."

Lucian's lips curved faintly, the expression polite but distant. "I'm certain the good doctor will find another puzzle soon."

The nurse chuckled, clearly missing the undercurrent in his tone. He reached to adjust one of the lines on the monitor, but Lucian's low and steady voice stopped him.

"That won't be necessary," he said. "I would prefer… privacy, for a moment."

The nurse blinked, thrown off by the subtle command in his tone. His eyes darted to Evelyn, as though expecting her to override it.

"It's fine," she said quietly. "I'll stay with him a while."

The man hesitated, then nodded, the authority in Lucian's presence leaving little room for argument. "Right. Call if you need anything."

When the door clicked shut behind him, the quiet returned, although thicker this time, edged with something almost electric.

Evelyn turned to Lucian, crossing her arms as though to steady herself. "You really shouldn't talk to staff like that," she said, her voice measured. "They're only trying to help."

Lucian tilted his head, studying her. "Help," he repeated softly, as if testing the word. "You think that's what they do here?"

She frowned, unsure whether he was mocking her or genuinely curious. "That's what hospitals are for. To keep people alive."

A pause stretched between them. The rain whispered against the windows.

Lucian's gaze drifted to the skyline beyond, the faint light of Crescent City bleeding into the clouds. "Alive," he echoed, almost to himself. "You say that as if it's something simple."

Evelyn's heartbeat, or what passed for it, seemed to thrum louder in her ears.

"What are you talking about?" she asked.

Lucian turned back to her, his expression unreadable. The faint light caught in his eyes again, silver bright.

"There's something you deserve to know," he said quietly. "About who I am… and why I'm here."

Lucian's gaze lingered on Evelyn, searching her face as if weighing how much truth she could bear. The monitors pulsed steadily beside him. His heartbeat is strong now, steady in a way that felt impossible just days ago.

He drew in a slow breath, the faintest tremor threading through it. "My name," he began, voice low but deliberate, "is not the one written on your intake forms."

Evelyn's brow furrowed. "You used an alias?"

"An old habit," he said, eyes drifting to the window where the rain traced slow paths down the glass. "Necessary for someone in my position."

There was gravity in his tone, like centuries of weight pressed into the space between syllables. Evelyn stepped closer, arms folding loosely, the distance between them charged but fragile. "Then what *is* your position, exactly?"

Lucian's lips quirked in something that might've been a smile, though it carried no amusement. "Lucian Devereaux," he said softly. "Crown Prince of the Court of Night."

The name fell between them like an unfamiliar and yet ancient spell stirring something deep in her memory, something she couldn't name.

Evelyn blinked, disbelief flashing across her face. "Prince," she echoed, the word tasting absurd in the sterile glow of the recovery suite. "You're telling me there's a *royal court* for..."

"For what I am," he finished, voice edged with exhaustion. "For what you are, too, though you may not have realized how closely our worlds are entwined."

Her throat tightened. The storm outside cracked faintly, lightning spilling across his features for an instant. "You don't expect me to believe that."

"I don't *need* you to," Lucian said quietly, the silver in his eyes brightening for a fleeting heartbeat. "But it's time you understood that our meeting was not a coincidence."

He leaned back against the pillows, every movement deliberate, controlled. "Fate has a cruel sense of timing, Evelyn. It tends to find those who try hardest to hide."

Evelyn stood frozen, her pulse quickening in her throat. The thunder rolled again, low and resonant, like some vast creature stirring above the city.

Lucian's gaze followed the lightning's reflection across the ceiling before returning to her. "You've heard the stories, haven't you?" he said softly. "Of the old bloodlines. The ones who ruled before the covens fractured. Before the hunger took dominion over reason."

"I've heard… whispers," Evelyn replied cautiously. "Legends, really. Nothing I ever believed."

Lucian nodded faintly. "They were true once. And now those truths are dying, piece by piece, rotting from within." His voice carried a strange calm, the tone of someone reciting his own obituary.

He pressed a hand lightly against his chest where the faint, spiral-like sigil had once flared. "My family's blood is poisoned, Evelyn. A curse laid generations ago by those we wronged. It festers slowly through the royal line, like an insidious parasite through the ages. It kills not with speed, but certainty."

Her eyes darted to the monitors, where his vitals were steady, almost serene. "And yet you're alive."

"For now," he said, a bitter half-smile ghosting across his lips. "But every heir of Devereaux falls the same way. Their power consumes them. Their bond destroys whoever dares to share it."

Evelyn felt a chill ripple through her. "Bond?" she echoed.

Lucian's eyes flickered toward her wrist, the place where the sigil had burned into her skin that night in the trauma bay. "The curse feeds on connection," he murmured. "It devours love, loyalty, even chance alignment. Anyone who draws too near…" His gaze lingered on her, sorrowful. "They don't survive the binding."

The storm outside deepened, and for a moment, the monitors faltered beneath the thunder's vibration. Evelyn swallowed hard, feeling the truth coil in her gut like ice. "You're saying I'm…"

Lucian looked away before she could finish. His jaw tightened, and his next words came softer than the rain.

"You were meant to be drawn into this."

Lucian's shoulders sagged slightly, the tension in him dissolving into quiet resignation. For a long moment, he didn't speak. Only the sound of the rain against the tall windows filled the space between them.

When he finally looked at her again, the careful control in his expression had fractured. "I didn't come to this city by accident," he said. "I came because of a name whispered through the Courts. A legend, half-forgotten."

Evelyn frowned, uncertain. "What legend?"

Lucian's voice softened to near reverence. "The Mortal Healer. One born of human compassion but marked by immortal blood. A creature who could mend what no other power could touch. The one who could purify even the cursed veins of the royal line."

The words felt heavy, ancient, carrying an echo that seemed to vibrate through the air.

He drew a shaky breath. "The prophecy said she would be hidden in plain sight. That she would not know what she was until the cursed prince found her."

Evelyn's pulse thudded in her ears. "And you think that's…"

"I *know* it is," he interrupted gently, eyes locking on hers with a strange mixture of certainty and regret. "When you touched me in the trauma bay, my blood didn't consume you. It recognized you. The sigil proved it."

The memory flared between them, the mark burning on her wrist, the whisper of language neither could understand.

Lucian leaned forward slightly, the monitors casting soft green light across his features. "I came here searching for salvation, Evelyn Carter. And I found *you*."

The room felt smaller, air thick with storm and tension. Evelyn could hear her own heart, the hum of his aura thrumming beneath it like a second rhythm.

But beneath his words, she sensed something else… *fear*. Not of death, but of what hope might cost him.

Evelyn took an involuntary step back, the cool tile pressing through the soles of her shoes grounding her against the surge of disbelief that threatened to drown her. The stormlight flickered through the windows, brief flashes of silver that cut across Lucian's face, the prince who had somehow bled into her every thought.

"I don't understand," she murmured, shaking her head as if she could dislodge the truth he'd placed there. "You think I'm part of some prophecy? That I'm meant to… what? *Heal* you? Break a curse written before I was even born?"

Lucian's expression didn't change, though a faint sorrow shadowed his features. "You've already begun to," he said softly.

Her throat tightened. "That's impossible."

"Is it?" he countered. "You've felt the bond between us, the pull, the shared mark. That's not invention, Evelyn. That's fate waking."

His words struck something inside her she didn't want to name. Because she *had* felt it every time he spoke her name, every time his aura brushed against hers like an old memory.

But her mind rebelled, sifting through the teachings her sire's mentor, old Sister Mirielle, had once drilled into her. *Never believe in destiny. It's just hunger with better manners.*

Evelyn clenched her jaw. "You don't know what you're asking me to believe. I'm not some… saint in disguise, or ancient savior. I'm a nurse. A mistake that never should have survived the turning."

Lucian's silver-black eyes glinted faintly in the half-light. "And yet you still heal," he murmured.

The words stung because they rang true. She'd spent her life stitching together the broken pieces others left behind, like patients, coworkers, even herself. And now this man, this *prince*, was telling her it meant something more.

Evelyn's pulse thundered in her ears. "If what you say is true," she whispered, "then why me?"

Lucian's lips parted, but he didn't answer… not yet.

Lucian's silence was more telling than any confession. The air between them thickened, charged with something neither of them dared to name. The rain softened to a whisper against the glass, and in the dim pulse of the monitors, Evelyn could hear both their hearts; his, slow and resonant; hers, stuttering beneath the weight of what he'd revealed.

When he finally spoke, his voice was quiet, stripped of its royal veneer. "Because you were never meant to heal me, Evelyn," he said. "You were meant to *choose* whether I deserve to be healed."

The words struck her harder than any truth yet revealed. His gaze held hers, raw and unguarded, and she felt the magnetic pull and the dangerous gravity of something ancient stirring between them again.

Part of her ached to reach for him, to understand the strange warmth that had begun threading through her veins since their fates intertwined. But another part, the disciplined and terrified part, remembered what intimacy cost creatures like them. What *bonds* destroyed.

She took a half step back, though her body betrayed her by trembling toward him. "You don't understand what you're asking," she said, voice breaking around the words. "If what you say is true, then being near you could kill us both."

Lucian's eyes dimmed, though his smile was gentle, resigned. "I've known that from the beginning."

The storm's reflection shimmered in the glass, lightning painting their faces in brief, ghostly light. Evelyn felt her control unraveling; her heart and hunger and fear tangling into something she couldn't name.

She turned toward the window, unable to face him fully, her reflection a pale echo beside his. "Then maybe," she whispered, "we should've never met."

Behind her, Lucian's reply came like a soft and inevitable vow. "And yet, we did."

The monitors hummed on, steady and indifferent, as the weight of prophecy and desire settled between them like a breath held too long, neither willing to break it.

Chapter 9

Prophecy's Echo

The stairwell to the hospital's lower levels groaned beneath Evelyn's steps, each creak echoing off the concrete like a warning. The scent of disinfectant faded with every descent, replaced by the heavier perfume of dust and time. When she pushed through the final steel door, the air turned thick and stale with decades of neglect.

The archives stretched before her in a dim sprawl of shadow and decay. Old metal shelving bowed under the weight of forgotten ledgers, medical charts yellowed to parchment, and stacks of brittle photographs curling at the edges. A single fluorescent tube flickered overhead, buzzing like a trapped insect.

Evelyn pulled her lab coat tighter, her fingers brushing the faint warmth of the sigil hidden beneath her sleeve. She didn't entirely know what she was looking for, only that she couldn't ignore the pull. The same restless hum that had haunted her since the night Lucian spoke the word *prophecy*.

She moved between the shelves, dust motes swirling in her wake like pale fireflies. Faded labels marked the years: *1912. 1889. 1861.* Her steps slowed at that last one.

A rusted placard read: St. Augustine Charity Ward Naval Infirmary Records.

Her pulse kicked up. That was the hospital's first incarnation. The hospital was built during the blockade years, when Crescent City had been little more than a harbor of smugglers and soldiers. She hesitated only a moment before prying open the brittle clasp of a leather-bound ledger.

Inside, the ink had bled and browned, but the handwriting was elegant, looping in the manner of a careful scholar. She traced the words with a gloved fingertip, deciphering fragments of ship manifests, injury tallies… and then something else.

A sigillum de noctis et sanguine, sign of night and blood.

Evelyn froze. The phrase pulsed in her mind like a heartbeat.

Her breath caught as she turned another brittle page. Ink and mildew filled the air as though time itself seemed to seep from the parchment. She flipped through page after page, skimming the terse notations of injuries and deaths, the language clinical yet haunting: *gunshot to lung, infection advanced, patient refused morphine—screamed hymns until dawn.*

But deeper in the stack, something shifted. The ledgers gave way to thinner volumes, bound in cracked leather and labeled in faint, fading ink. JOURNAL OF DR. J. MERCER, 1861–1865.

Evelyn slid one free. The spine groaned, and dust curled like breath in the lamplight. Inside, the tone changed. The journal was less administrative and more personal. *Charity ward now serves blockade runners and wounded mariners. Supplies low. Disease rampant. Yet among the dying, one stranger endures; skin cold, wounds unhealed yet bloodless. Says he bears the mark of the night prince.*

Her pulse quickened. She turned the page, faster now, until she found sketches. They were rough pencil etchings of a spiral intertwined with thorns, the same sigil she'd seen glowing on Lucian's chest. The same one that appeared on her wrist. Beneath it, the doctor's scrawl: *A curse or covenant? The symbol burned upon both healer and afflicted.*

Her fingers trembled as she traced the lines, recognition flaring like lightning through her.

The next journal confirmed the pattern. More entries and more whispers of something unnatural entwined with the hospital's history.

The patient claims prophecy binds his blood to hers. She is the healer who drinks from no living man. Together they shall mend the wound of night or perish by it.

Evelyn's eyes flicked upward as thunder rolled faintly above, even down here beneath the earth. For the first time, she felt the hospital's age pressing in, as if it's very foundations were listening.

She swallowed hard, the sigil on her wrist tingling faintly through the glove. "What were you, Dr. Mercer?" she whispered. "And what did you find?"

Evelyn stepped back from the shelf, clutching the fragile journal to her chest as she fished her phone from her coat pocket. The screen's pale glow cut through the gloom, throwing her reflection against the glass of a dusty cabinet. Her eyes were shadowed, hair tangled, looking more like a ghost than a nurse.

She hesitated for a heartbeat, then opened the browser and typed: "Dr. Josiah Mercer Crescent City 1860s."

For a moment, nothing. Then, slowly, fragments surfaced from digital archives and university databases. She found scraps of old newspapers, historical society records, and forgotten obituaries.

"Local physician accused of spiritualist delusions." "Dr. J. Mercer dismissed from St. Augustine's Infirmary following public claims of vampiric infection among wounded sailors." "Died 1883, Crescent City poorhouse. No family, no visitors."

Evelyn's stomach turned as she scrolled through the brittle scans of yellowed clippings. One grainy photograph caught her eye: a stern-faced man with intelligent, haunted eyes, standing in front of the very same arched windows that now overlooked Lucian's recovery room.

He believed in us, she thought grimly. *And they destroyed him for it.*

Another headline made her breath hitch.

"Disgraced doctor publishes banned pamphlet: 'On the Dual Nature of the Living Dead.'"

She tapped through, the text blurry but legible enough to make out one chilling line:

"Blood remembers what the body forgets. In every generation, the healer and the afflicted will meet again, until the curse is unmade or renewed."

Evelyn stared at the words, her pulse thudding in her throat. The hum beneath her skin, the one that had been growing since Lucian's arrival, seemed to vibrate in recognition.

She shut off the phone, plunging the room back into the dull glow of the single fluorescent light. The walls seemed to lean closer, the air thick with memory.

"Josiah Mercer," she whispered into the stillness. "What did you start?"

Evelyn slid her phone back into her pocket and exhaled slowly, forcing her thoughts to still. The silence pressed close, punctuated only by the soft hum of the light and the occasional drip of condensation from a rusted pipe.

She turned her attention back to the shelves, drawn toward a cluster of wooden boxes stacked haphazardly beneath a sagging row of ledgers. Their labels were half-faded, the ink eaten away by time: ARCHIVE B – CHARITY WARD / PERSONAL EFFECTS.

Crouching, she brushed away the thick layer of dust and pried open one of the boxes. Inside lay a jumble of folded parchment, water-damaged envelopes, and wax-sealed folders stamped with the hospital's early insignia. The scent of old paper and iron hit her like a smell so dense with age it was almost metallic.

Her gloved hands moved carefully, sorting through brittle fragments of correspondence: letters between physicians, patient rosters, shipping manifests for medical supplies smuggled past Union blockades. The ink on one page had bled from black to rust red. *All blood returns to the sea*, someone had scrawled in the margin.

Another document caught her eye. It was a sheaf of loose sketches bound with a thin leather cord. She drew them out and unfolded the top sheet. Her breath caught in her chest.

There it was again.

A spiral entwined with thorns, drawn over and over in different variations; some small and intricate, others large enough to fill the page. In the center of one sketch, faded but still legible, someone had inked a phrase in Latin beneath the sigil. The handwriting was careful, reverent, as if transcribing scripture.

Evelyn tilted the page toward the light. The words were unfamiliar, but one term leapt out like a wound reopened: *sanguinem principis*.

The blood of the prince.

She swallowed hard and reached deeper into the box. More pages followed, filled with the same looping script, dense Latin passages interspersed with rough anatomical drawings; veins, hearts, and what appeared to be ritual markings across the chest and wrist.

Her gloved fingers trembled as she laid the papers out in the dim glow, the storm outside rumbling faintly through the pipes overhead.

Whatever this was, it wasn't just superstition or folklore. It was *recorded*. Studied. Remembered.

Evelyn stared down at the sigil. The same one that had burned into her flesh.

It was waiting to be understood.

Evelyn gathered the sketches and spread them across the nearest metal cart, its surface cold beneath her palms. The pages shivered faintly in the draft that sighed through the vents, the Latin words half-obscured by stains and the ghostly touch of time.

She leaned close, pulling her phone back out to use its flashlight. The light caught the raised texture of the ink, which was handwritten, not printed, suggesting a ritual text, not a clinical record. She whispered the words aloud, slow and careful, tasting their shape.

"Sanctum sanguinem… medicus mortalis… princeps noctis…"

Her rudimentary Latin struggled to keep pace, but fragments began to coalesce in her mind. *Holy blood… mortal healer… prince of night.*

The verses were structured like a litany; part prayer, part incantation. She flipped to the next page, and there, beneath another rendering of the thorned spiral, was a longer passage.

Cum sanguis et lumen conveniant, Vinculum fit inter vivos et noctem. Sanabit quod est fractum, Aut mundo novam pestem dabit.

Her eyes narrowed, translating by instinct and the echo of old church Latin Sister Mirielle had once forced her to memorize:

When blood and light converge, A bond is forged between life and night. It shall heal what is broken, Or bring a new plague upon the world.

A shiver rippled through her. The sigil seemed to shimmer faintly under the phone's light like *an illusion of ink*, she told herself, nothing more.

However, she couldn't shake the feeling that the text was more than a prophecy. She felt like it was a *ritual.* A set of instructions meant to be followed.

She flipped to another sketch: two figures facing each other, their wrists joined over a vessel, the spiral etched between their hearts. The notation beneath was sharp and deliberate, written in English this time:

Union demands blood freely given. Trust beyond fear, and pain embraced as a covenant.

Evelyn drew back, her stomach tightening. The idea of a ritual that bound healer and prince, *her* and Lucian, was almost too much to comprehend.

The sigil beneath her glove throbbed once, a subtle pulse that felt like an answer.

Evelyn's fingers trembled as she turned another page, revealing a series of meticulous diagrams, unsettling in their precision. The drawings looked like a physician's work, but the subject matter had slipped beyond medicine into something darker. Something older.

Each illustration paired anatomy with symbology: a heart encircled by thorns; veins marked with runes that mirrored the spiral's curvature; and written notes that read like both an invocation and a warning.

She steadied the beam of her phone's light over one page in particular. It showed two figures kneeling opposite one another, their forearms slashed and pressed together over a shallow basin carved with the sigil. Beneath it, in slanted English script:

The healer gives of the mortal vein; the prince of night returns in kind. Only through shared pain shall corruption be purged.

The next passage went further, the handwriting growing more fevered.

If trust falters, the bond turns upon them both. The light devours the night, or the night consumes the light. Thus, the balance is kept.

Evelyn exhaled slowly, the words etching themselves into her thoughts. Sacrifice and trust. Not ritual ingredients, but emotional absolutes. A covenant written in blood and intent.

Another document lay folded beneath, sealed once with wax that had long since flaked away. She opened it carefully. This one was a personal account, written in the same neat script she recognized from Dr. Mercer's journal.

The union cannot be forced. The healer must give freely; the prince must restrain his nature. Should one falter, death binds them both, and the curse renews. Yet if both endure…

The ink smeared there, possibly due to water damage or something else. The sentence trailed off into a spatter that looked disturbingly like blood.

Evelyn's pulse pounded in her temples. She skimmed through more fragments of notations of attempts made, of failure after failure. Each ended the same way: *subject expired.*

One line, written near the bottom margin, stopped her cold.

Perhaps the prophecy was never meant to be fulfilled. Perhaps it was a warning disguised as hope.

She stared at the words until her eyes blurred. The sigil on her wrist throbbed again, harder this time, as though it recognized what she'd just read.

The storm rumbled far above, but down here, beneath stone and shadow, Evelyn could almost feel the city's heartbeat aligning with her own; fast, fearful, and thrumming with revelation.

Evelyn sank back onto the cold concrete floor, the papers scattered around her like fallen leaves from another century. The faint glow from the fluorescent bulb overhead painted everything in shades of rust and omen. She pressed a hand to her wrist, feeling the pulse of that strange warmth beneath her skin; a heartbeat that wasn't quite hers.

For so long, she'd believed her turning had been meaningless. A cruel accident. A punishment. But now, staring at the proof of prophecy. She felt like her name was written between the lines of history. She felt the faint pull of purpose threading through the fear. *The healer of blood and the prince of night.*

Her chest ached with something that wasn't quite hope. If this prophecy were true, then maybe her suffering meant something. Maybe her existence wasn't just survival. Maybe it was part of something larger, something ancient.

And yet, that same thought hollowed her out.

What if Lucian hadn't found her by chance? What if every heartbeat, every glance, every night spent at his bedside had been scripted centuries before? A cruel hand of fate is tightening around them both.

She looked at the sigil again, traced the thorns with a trembling fingertip. Its meaning whispered of devotion and ruin in the same breath.

"I won't be used," she murmured into the still air, though her voice shook.

The vow rang hollow, even to her own ears. Because beneath the defiance, something deeper stirred; a longing not for freedom, but for understanding. For him.

The thought terrified her more than any prophecy could.

Chapter 10

Hunter's Net

The night pressed against St. Augustine's Hospital like a living thing. It was restless and thick with the taste of metal and rain. Wind clawed at the tall palms that lined the courtyard, scattering wet leaves across the asphalt. Somewhere beyond the ambulance bay, thunder rolled low and hungry, rattling the old iron gutters.

A sudden flash of lightning split the clouds, momentarily bleaching the world in white before plunging it back into darkness. Then, the floodlights stuttered and steadied into a feverish flicker that painted the walls in fits of pallid gold.

Overhead, the emergency sirens let out a mechanical groan, followed by the soft hiss of the intercom. "Attention all staff. Security lockdown protocol is now in effect. This is a drill. Please remain in your assigned areas until further notice."

Metal doors sealed with hydraulic sighs. The automatic gates in the parking lot groaned shut, cutting off the world beyond. From the upper floors, Evelyn watched the lights wink out across the campus one by one, until only the red glow of exit signs and the pulse of backup generators remained.

She felt the shift, not just in the air pressure, but in the rhythm of the place. Hospitals had their own heartbeat. A cadence of movement and machinery, and tonight that rhythm faltered. Beneath the hum of the generators, she sensed something else. She sensed a wrongness, coiled and waiting.

The storm was only a mask for something colder moving through the night.

The rumor spread faster than the rain against the windows. First it was a whisper at the nurse's station, something about intruders near the west entrance, armed and dangerous. Then it was on everyone's lips, carried down the corridors like an infection no one wanted to name. The "security drill" story unraveled within minutes.

Evelyn stood by the medication cart in the dim red light of the emergency backup system, listening to the tension sharpen the air. Even the machines seemed quieter, as if the hospital itself was holding its breath.

Mateo burst through the double doors with his usual swagger, his scrubs half untucked and a grin just barely concealing his unease. "Armed intruders? Please. The only thing dangerous around here is the coffee in the staff lounge."

A few nurses tried to laugh, though it came out strained and brittle. One of them, a tired charge nurse with mascara smudged under her eyes, muttered, "If this is a drill, I'm quitting. Again."

Mateo leaned casually against the counter, twirling a pen like it was a baton. "Relax, chichas. If someone's stupid enough to break into a hospital, they deserve whatever tetanus shot they're gonna get."

That earned him a few nervous chuckles, and even Evelyn found the corner of her mouth twitching. But beneath his playful tone, she caught the faint tremor in his heartbeat, the way his gaze kept darting toward the sealed exits.

The humidity outside built thicker, fogging the windows in their frames. Somewhere down the hall, a door slammed. Evelyn's senses prickled beyond the laughter, beyond the fear; something deliberate moved through the dark.

Evelyn's smile faded the moment Mateo looked away. The hum of fluorescent lights dimmed, replaced by the low, electric thrum of her instincts. Something was wrong. The lockdown wasn't about safety drills or stray intruders; it was *targeted*. She could feel it in the rhythm of the building, in the way every vent, every hum of electricity seemed to vibrate with anticipation.

"Evelyn," a voice said softly.

Dr. Meredith Kwon stood beside her, clipboard in hand, expression calm but alert. The attending's dark eyes missed nothing, least of all Evelyn's rigid posture and the faint twitch of her jaw.

"You're wound tighter than the IV lines," Meredith murmured, keeping her tone light enough for the nearby nurses not to notice. "Deep breaths. It's probably just another false alarm."

Mateo snorted. "False alarm? Please. Last time it was a raccoon in the supply closet. I'm telling you, that thing had murder in its eyes."

Meredith didn't even look at him. "Mateo," she said dryly, "if you can't tell the difference between wildlife and workplace hazards, I'm scheduling you for another safety seminar."

That got a small ripple of laughter from the others. It was thin and nervous, but it was laughter, nonetheless. Evelyn appreciated the distraction, but it barely reached her. Her focus was elsewhere. It was on the distant cadence of voices echoing faintly through her sharpened hearing.

They were not voices from this floor. Not staff.

The tone was clipped, coded. Syllables broken in a pattern she half-recognized from whispers in her old world. *Hunter chatter.*

Evelyn's pulse didn't race. It stopped, caught in the space between heartbeats.

The fragments of speech crackled faintly through the static hum of the hospital's intercom system, indistinct at first, then sharper as Evelyn focused her senses.

"Unit four, confirm west wing cleared."
"Negative. Target movement is possible. Eyes on sublevel access." "Copy. Proceed with stake protocol."

Her blood chilled. No mistaking it now. *Stake protocol.* Hunters. Here, inside St. Augustine's.

She forced her expression into something neutral, aware that Dr. Kwon was watching her. The older woman's gaze was perceptive, steady as steel under her calm exterior.

"Carter," Dr. Kwon said, her voice cutting through the tense silence. "You and Mateo need to take a portable cooler from the supply, Group B blood units, and a sedative tray, to Mr. Devereaux's room. They're rerouting all critical inventory in case of power loss."

Evelyn blinked, refocusing. "Now?"

"Yes, now." Meredith's tone left no room for debate. "We're short-staffed, and he's a priority patient. Take the east corridor; the west side's been sealed."

Mateo straightened from where he'd been leaning against the counter, his usual smirk faltering. "Wait, sealed? As in... locked down sealed?"

Dr. Kwon gave him a reassuring pat on the arm. "It's precautionary, Mateo. You'll both be fine." Then, lower, almost too low for human ears, she added, "Stick together."

The words hit Evelyn as a whisper threaded with meaning. *Stick together.*

She met Kwon's eyes briefly and saw something there. A flicker of understanding. The doctor didn't know everything, but she *knew enough.*

Evelyn nodded slowly. "Understood."

A racket rolled above the hospital floor, shaking the windowpanes as emergency lights pulsed along the hall like a heartbeat. Somewhere beneath that rhythm, Evelyn could still hear the hunters' coded chatter tightening its net around them.

Evelyn and Mateo pushed a supply cart down the narrow corridor, the wheels creaking softly against the linoleum. The emergency lights cast long red shadows that flickered with every gust of wind rattling the hospital windows. She kept one hand on the cooler, steadying the contents: blood units for Lucian, sedatives, and a small med kit just in case.

Mateo hummed under his breath, trying to mask the tension with a playful tone. "You know, if we survive tonight, I vote for chocolate and margaritas. Preferably both at once."

Evelyn allowed herself a small, tight-lipped smile, though her senses remained alert. The faint click of distant boots made her spine prickle. The weather outside and the hunters inside created a rhythm that made every step echo like a drumbeat.

Suddenly, Mateo's pager buzzed sharply at his hip. He glanced down, his smile faltering. "Duty calls," he muttered, eyes widening. "Code blue in ICU. You're on your own for Lucian."

"Alone?" Evelyn asked, her voice low. She glanced down the corridor, the red glow painting the walls in ominous hues.

Mateo gave her a brief, apologetic shrug. "Hey, you've handled worse than this. And I know your little microphone ears are picking up things I don't even want to think about."

Evelyn exhaled, swallowing the nervous energy that had knotted in her chest. "Just be careful," she said, her tone softer than she intended.

Mateo offered a half-grin, then vanished down the nearest stairwell, leaving her standing beside the supply cart in the flickering red light.

Alone, Evelyn adjusted her grip on the cart, listening to the faint hum of the backup generators and the distant, coded chatter still threading through the building. Every instinct screamed for caution, but there was no turning back now.

She took a deep breath and started down the corridor toward Lucian's room, wheels creaking softly beneath her as the night and the hunters' invisible presence closed in around her.

Evelyn's footsteps were measured, almost soundless, as she guided the cart down the shadowed corridors. The emergency lights flickered overhead, throwing brief, erratic illuminations that made the walls seem to sway and pulse. Every reflection in the glossy floor tiles or the darkened windows felt like it might be a watcher, every distant sound a footstep not her own.

She slowed at a corner, pressing her back against the wall, listening. The faint metallic clink of boots echoed somewhere ahead. They were too methodical to be an imagination-driven distraction. Her instincts flared. These weren't hospital security staff. They moved with purpose, scanning, testing exits, and counting. Hunters.

Evelyn held her breath, letting the red light wash over her skin like a protective cloak. She adjusted the cart's trajectory, sliding it into a shadowed alcove just as a patrol rounded the corner. The figures were broad-shouldered, dressed in dark jackets and security vests, their faces obscured by caps and masks. One paused, then shrugged to a companion, and they moved on, unaware of her presence.

The metallic scent of their weapons carried faintly to her, mingling with the sharp tang of antiseptic and her own heightened awareness. She let the pulse of her own heartbeat slow, letting her vampire senses map the corridors; vent shafts, emergency exits, and blind spots. All the paths she could use to avoid contact.

She exhaled slowly and nudged the cart forward, leaning low and hugging the walls. Every creak of the wheels sounded like an alarm in her ears, every shadow a potential threat. When another patrol passed by a junction ahead, she froze again, letting them move first, her body pressed against the cool wall, waiting for the footsteps to fade.

The slow wind outside rattled the windows, punctuating each tense moment with a deafening rattle of glass and metal. It was as if the night itself was conspiring with her senses, masking her presence while the hunters swept past.

Step by careful step, she inched closer to Lucian's room, each movement deliberate, silent, and rehearsed in her mind a dozen times over. The hospital had transformed into a maze of danger, but she could feel the faint pulse of the room ahead, faint but steady, guiding her toward him.

Evelyn rounded the final corner, her body pressed low against the wall, cart wheels whispering against the linoleum. Ahead, the faint green glow of Lucian's heart monitor filtered under the door, steady and familiar, a beacon in the chaotic night.

The patrols had shifted further down the hall, their boots echoing elsewhere, but she knew they were still close, hunters moving like shadows, sweeping the hospital with methodical intent. Every instinct screamed caution, every muscle tensed for flight or fight.

She knelt briefly behind the cart, taking a measured breath. The lights overhead flickered, and somewhere distant, the coded chatter of hunters pulsed faintly, like the echo of a predator's heartbeat.

Her fingers brushed the handle of the cart, steadying herself. Lucian was just beyond that door, waiting, unaware of how close danger had come. Evelyn's mind sharpened, calculating the approach, mapping each potential threat, every safe step in the gauntlet between her and him.

With one last glance down the corridor, she pushed the cart forward, the hum of the generators and the storm merging with her heightened senses as she neared his room, every fiber of her being alert and poised for what came next.

Evelyn paused just outside Lucian's door, the cart resting silently beside her. Every corridor behind her seemed to close in, the flickering red emergency lights throwing long, uncertain shadows that shifted with each gust of wind rattling the windows.

Somewhere in the bowels of the hospital, hunters moved with deliberate stealth, their patrols threading through the maze of corridors and stairwells. One wrong step or one careless nudge of the cart, or one inadvertent sound could betray them both.

The familiar hum of the generators and the faint beeping of monitors blended into a tense symphony of anticipation. Evelyn's senses stretched to their limits, mapping every shadow, every vent, every potential path of pursuit. The hospital had transformed into a living trap, claustrophobic and labyrinthine, and she felt the weight of responsibility pressing down on her shoulders.

Her heart, steady in its human rhythm yet quickened by her vampiric attunement, reminded her that Lucian's safety rested entirely in her hands. That one misstep here could doom them both.

The room loomed before her, a fragile sanctuary in a storm of threat, and with a slow, controlled breath, lyn crossed the threshold

Chapter 11

Blood Oath

The blackout still held the hospital in its grip. Only the wavering light of candles stolen from the chapel downstairs illuminated Lucian's recovery room. Their flames danced across the sterile steel and white tile, softening everything they touched into gold and shadow. The faint scent of melted wax mingled with antiseptic, an odd alchemy of sacred and clinical.

Evelyn stood by the window, watching the storm drag its fingers down the glass. Beyond the panes, the city was a blur of lightning and drowned neon. Inside, the silence pressed close. The generators had failed again, and even the monitors had gone dark, save for a dim, faltering pulse that matched the beat of her own heart.

Lucian lay propped against the pillows, his skin pale but his gaze alert, watching her with eyes that seemed too old for his face. A candle on the bedside tray threw a thin halo around him, and the sight stirred something unsteady in her chest. Was it fear? Yes, but also recognition, that same pulse of connection she had tried so hard to ignore.

She turned at last, the sound of her movement soft against the hush. "You shouldn't be sitting up yet," she murmured, defaulting to her nurse's instinct even as she sensed he was stronger than he appeared.

Lucian gave a small, tired smile. "Perhaps. But time is no longer something I can afford to obey."

The candlelight caught the faint glint of something metallic at his throat. It was an old crest on a chain, the same spiral-and-thorn motif she had seen burned into his skin. His voice, though quiet, carried a gravity that filled the room, as though even the storm outside paused to listen.

Evelyn's unease deepened. The air itself seemed to thicken, as if what he was about to say might alter more than the night, it might alter *them*.

Evelyn moved closer to the bedside, the hem of her scrub pants whispering against the tile. The candlelight threw fractured reflections on the window, where the storm still prowled like a restless animal.

"Power's been down for hours," she said quietly, checking the still-dark monitors by habit. "Backups keep failing. Even the lockdown doors are running on emergency circuits."

Lucian followed her gaze to the flickering glass, where a bolt of lightning carved a jagged scar across the skyline. "The storm will pass," he murmured, his tone distant, almost resigned. "But what comes after storms always leaves something broken."

Evelyn frowned, unsure if he meant the weather or something else entirely. "You make it sound like the building won't still be standing by morning."

A faint curve touched his lips. "Perhaps not *everything* built to last deserves to survive the night."

She crossed her arms, leaning slightly against the counter where the candles burned low. "The lockdown's still active. They said it's just a drill, but…" Her voice trailed off, the unease pressing tighter against her ribs.

Lucian's eyes lifted to hers. "But you don't believe them."

Evelyn shook her head slowly. "No. I can *feel* it. It's like the walls are listening. Like the air's waiting for something."

He regarded her in silence for a long moment, and when he finally spoke, his voice had dropped to a quiet, intimate register. "You're not wrong. You were never meant to be."

The words sent a chill down her spine, threading through the heat of the candles and the pulse of the storm outside.

"Lucian…" she began, the question forming before she could stop it, "what exactly is happening tonight?"

He looked toward the window again, lightning flashing across his pale profile. He was composed, almost mournful. When he turned back to her, his expression had hardened into quiet resolve.

"Something I've kept at bay too long," he said softly. "And something I can no longer hide."

Lucian's eyes drifted toward the candle flames, their reflections trembling across the sheen of sweat on his temple. For a long moment, he said nothing, and Evelyn could hear only the rain against the glass and the faint, unsteady rhythm of his breathing.

When he finally spoke, his voice was quiet and measured; however, every syllable carried the weight of confession. "It's begun," he murmured. "The curse. What sleeps in my blood has awakened."

Evelyn's breath caught. "You mean… what you told me before? The illness?"

Lucian shook his head faintly. "Illness implies something that can be cured by mortal means. This is older. A rot passed from king to heir, from crown to crown, until the very blood that sustains us turns against its own vessel." He lifted a trembling hand, pressing it over his chest, where beneath skin and bandages the faint sigil still pulsed like living ink. "It's feeding now. Each hour it devours more of me."

Evelyn's medical instincts surged forward even as her reason faltered. "Then we need a transfusion, something…"

"It won't help." His voice sharpened, cutting through her words. "The curse rejects all mortal blood. There is only one thing that can slow its hunger."

He met her gaze, and the air between them seemed to tighten, charged with something both electric and ancient. "A *blood-bond ritual*," he said at last, the phrase landing between them like a verdict. "Forbidden among our kind because it ties two souls until death cannot tell them apart."

Evelyn felt her pulse thrum in her throat. "You mean… sharing blood."

Lucian nodded once, slowly. "Yes. My blood and yours. It would grant me strength enough to resist the curse, for a time. But it would not come without consequence."

The candles guttered in a sudden draft, their flames bowing low as if the very room recoiled from his words. Evelyn's hands, still clasped before her, trembled. She wanted to step back, to put distance between them, but something in his gaze rooted her in place.

Lucian's eyes flickered toward the flickering candlelight again, as though drawing strength from the dim, shifting glow. When he spoke, his voice had changed to a lower and steadier tone. It seemed touched by the cadence of ancient memory.

"The ritual is not performed in words alone," he said, gaze returning to her. "It demands intention. A vow spoken not to gods or to fate, but to the blood itself."

He shifted, the faintest wince betraying his exhaustion, and extended a hand toward her. His fingers were pale, elegant, trembling slightly from the effort. "First, there must be a circle," he continued. "Blood drawn from both participants. It must be mingled over an open flame. This symbolizes the first breath, the first spark that separates life from death."

Evelyn listened, half in disbelief, half in fascination, the air between them charged with something close to reverence.

"Then," Lucian said, voice soft but deliberate, "the blood is shared. Each must drink of the other, willingly, while naming the bond aloud. The vow must bind *life to life*, not power to power, not hunger to hunger. If there is deceit in the heart of either, the circle burns black, and both perish."

His words fell like the toll of distant bells, ancient and inevitable. Evelyn's mouth had gone dry. "You've… done this before?" she whispered.

Lucian's eyes darkened, shadows gliding across their violet hue. "Never," he said. "It was forbidden, even for those of royal blood. To attempt it without purity of purpose was to invite madness or worse. But the curse leaves me no choice."

He looked down, his hand curling slowly into a fist against his thigh. "If we begin, the circle must not be broken until both have spoken the vow. Not by fear. Not by hesitation. Once started... it cannot be undone."

The candles flared suddenly, wax dripping onto the tray beside the bed. The silence that followed was as fragile as spun glass. Evelyn's pulse thundered in her ears.

Lucian's gaze held hers, unflinching, as if reading the turmoil in her thoughts. He let the silence stretch, letting the weight of the storm outside and the flickering candlelight fill the room, before speaking again.

"The effect is immediate, subtle, and irreversible," he said, voice low, measured. "Once the bond is formed, our life forces intertwine. Your heartbeat will echo in mine, my pulse in yours. Injuries, sickness, and exhaustion all will be shared, as if we were two halves of a single body."

He lifted a trembling hand to his chest, tracing the faint spiral-thorn sigil beneath the bandages. "Pain will be doubled at first," he admitted, "but strength comes in equal measure. You will sense what I sense, feel what I feel, not just for a moment, but for the span of our lives."

Evelyn's stomach tightened. "Lives? What do you mean?"

"The bond is more than flesh," he said, turning slightly to catch the candlelight across his pale cheek. "It's spirit as well. One cannot exist without the other. Should you die, I will follow. And should I fall… you will be claimed by the same fate. Our essences, our very blood, tethered beyond hope of separation."

She swallowed hard, the words lodging in her throat. The warmth of the candlelight, the scent of wax and antiseptic, and the quiet hum of the storm outside seemed to shrink the room around her.

"Do you understand what you're asking?" Lucian's violet eyes bore into hers, intense and patient, yet tinged with the same vulnerability she had glimpsed in him before.

Evelyn's hands clenched at her sides. She did understand. And the weight of that understanding made her heart pound faster than any danger outside these walls ever had.

Lucian leaned closer, the candlelight casting shadows across the sharp planes of his face. His voice softened, heavy with the gravity of what he was about to say.

"Evelyn," he whispered, and the name hung between them, intimate and insistent. "You must understand this is no mere transfusion. If you share your blood with me, we will be bound, irrevocably."

He lifted a pale hand, hovering over hers as if to emphasize the connection. "Your life will be tied to mine. Every pulse you feel, every beat of your heart, will resonate in me. And mine in you. Should you die, I die. Should I fall… You will follow."

The words pressed into her chest, heavier than the storm that battered the windows. The room seemed to shrink, the flickering candlelight exaggerating every shadow, every tremor in his tone.

"This is not a risk I take lightly," he continued, eyes searching hers, holding hers. "Nor is it one you should. But without it… the curse will claim me completely. And nothing, no mortal skill or medicine can stop it."

Evelyn swallowed hard, the ethical and emotional weight of his confession pressing down like stone. She could feel the potential consequences threading through her thoughts: the tethering of their lives, the exposure to the hunters outside, and the irreversibility of such a bond.

The storm outside roared, a low echo of the storm raging in her own chest.

Evelyn pressed her palms to her face, trying to steady her breath, the candlelight throwing her reflection across the walls in fractured, wavering shadows. Her mind spun with the gravity of his words.

To help him… to willingly entwine her life with his, she would sacrifice the careful balance she had maintained since her turning. Her humanity, already fragile, could be eroded in an instant by the intimate sharing of blood with a vampire whose existence defied every law she had once sworn to uphold.

And the hunters. They were still out there, moving like ghosts through the hospital, attuned to the faintest scent of vampiric blood. Any exposure or any misstep could lead them straight to Lucian. And by extension to her. The weight of responsibility pressed down, thick and suffocating, a storm within a storm.

Her mind flickered back to the nights she had restrained herself from feeding, the lines she had drawn between instinct and morality. Crossing this line would not only risk her life, but it would also compromise everything she had fought to maintain since becoming what she was.

Yet, beneath that fear, a pulse of something else stirred: duty, perhaps, or inevitability. Her connection to Lucian, the bond she had felt from the first moment she sensed his aura, was not simply attraction. It was recognition, a call that had been whispering through her veins long before she understood its meaning.

Evelyn's hands tightened into fists at her sides. The ethical cost was immense, the danger unrelenting, and yet… her hesitation faltered under the gravity of the choice. To act or not to act? This decision would define the course of both their lives.

The candlelight flickered again, shadows crawling across the room like sentient fingers, and Evelyn felt the weight of destiny pressing down on her shoulders, unyielding and absolute.

Evelyn drew in a long, deliberate breath, the flickering candlelight warming her skin even as her pulse raced. Every instinct screamed caution, every shadow whispered of danger, yet beneath it all, a steady current of certainty began to thread through her thoughts.

She thought of the nights she had spent restraining herself, of the hunger she had mastered and the lives she had chosen not to take. She thought of the hunters lurking beyond these walls, and the knowledge that standing idle would not protect Lucian or herself.

And then she looked at him, vulnerable in a way that made her chest tighten. The connection she had felt since their first encounter and the echo of recognition in his presence surged through her veins like wildfire.

Her decision crystallized, unyielding and absolute. She would act. Not because fate demanded it, not because prophecy dictated it, but because she chose to. Because she would not stand aside while the man whose life had become entwined with hers suffered a fate she had the power to alter.

Evelyn squared her shoulders, stepping closer to the bedside. Her hands, steady despite the storm inside her, reached toward the tools and vials she would need. Fear and desire, duty and instinct, coalesced into resolve.

She met Lucian's gaze, and in that instant, the choice was no longer hypothetical. She would bind herself to him, tether their lives together, and face whatever consequences awaited them together.

The storm outside pounded the city, the candles flickered, and Evelyn Carter, once cautious, and reluctant, prepared to take a stand that would define everything that came after.

Evelyn's fingers hovered over the vials, her heartbeat steadying as the magnitude of her decision settled into her chest. The storm outside raged, the candlelight flickered, and yet in the quiet between the flashes of lightning, she felt a clarity she had never known.

For the first time since her turning, she was not merely surviving. She was choosing to act, to intervene, and stake her life. Not in fear or desperation, but in defiance of the forces that sought to control her.

The weight of hunters outside, the curse that threatened Lucian, the fragile thread of her own morality all pressed upon her, and still she stood firm.

This was no longer about reaction. This was about agency, about standing in the storm and taking a stand for something greater than herself.

Evelyn Carter exhaled slowly, her pulse steady, her resolve unbroken. She had stepped past hesitation and fear, and into a choice that would define her existence.

She was no longer a passive survivor. She was a force, willing to act and face whatever consequences awaited.

Chapter 12

Shadows in Scrubs

The staff lounge was a ghost of its usual self. It was dim and heavy with the scent of burnt coffee and antiseptic. The blackout had forced the hospital onto generator power again. This cast everything in a jaundiced amber glow. A single fluorescent tube buzzed near the ceiling, flickering at irregular intervals like a nervous pulse.

Outside the rain battered the windows, the storm's low growl vibrating through the walls. Inside, the hum of the backup generators mingled with the faint rattle of an air vent struggling to keep up. Stacks of paperwork sat abandoned on the counter beside a forgotten thermos, its contents long cold.

Down the short adjoining hallway, the medicine storage room loomed like a vault with rows of locked cabinets gleaming faintly in the emergency light. Metal shelves stood in orderly lines, labeled and precise, though the shadows between them seemed to breathe.

Evelyn lingered between the two spaces, the weight of sleepless nights pressing on her shoulders. The lounge, once a refuge for overworked staff, now felt claustrophobic. The faint hum of the vending machine and the steady patter of rain outside made her feel like she was being watched.

Something in the air had shifted since the lockdown. There was a tension that was too fine to name but impossible to ignore. Even the most mundane corners of the hospital seemed to hold their breath.

Evelyn eased into one of the creaking plastic chairs in the lounge, the kind that had molded to years of weary night-shift bodies. The table before her was littered with half-finished charts, a few loose pens, and a stack of papers someone had left in haste.

She pulled the stack closer, scanning the heading, which read "Staff Rotation & Security Access Logs – Night Shift". Her brow furrowed. These weren't the typical medical reports or patient charts she was used to finding here. The pages were stamped with timestamps, entry codes, and signature initials.

The rhythmic tick of the wall clock filled the silence, a metronome for her thoughts. She flipped through the first few pages, the faint scent of toner and coffee clinging to the sheets. The handwriting changed from line to line with familiar initials beside keycard numbers, late entries written in hurried strokes.

The flickering fluorescent light buzzed overhead again, briefly plunging the room into a flash of shadow before stabilizing. Evelyn exhaled slowly, tapping a pen against the table's edge. Something about the pages felt wrong. They felt too perfect in places, too conveniently aligned.

Her instincts, sharpened by sleepless nights and something deeper, whispered that these weren't just misplaced records. Someone had been here before her, editing, hiding, or planting something.

She leaned forward, elbows on the table, and began reading more carefully.

Evelyn flipped to the next page, her eyes narrowing as she traced a column of security access codes. The data should have been routine. There should have been timestamps aligning with staff rotations and badge swipes at controlled doors. However, a pattern began to emerge, subtle but unmistakable.

Certain codes repeated at irregular intervals, attached to shifts that didn't exist on the schedule she had helped post earlier in the week. Others bore initials of nurses, orderlies, and technicians she recognized. The times, however, logged made no sense. Some were marked during daylight hours when no one on the night team should've been on site. Others corresponded with the lockdown itself, moments when the system should've frozen all nonessential access.

A chill settled over her.

She cross-referenced a few of the entries with memory: Mateo's ID number, hers, Dr. Kwon's. They checked out. However, C. Reeves was listed twice within the same five-minute window. The logs show that ID swiping into two different wings of the hospital at once. Impossible. Unless someone had cloned her badge, or Clara herself had been helping the intruders.

Evelyn's pulse quickened. Beneath the familiar staff codes were newer entries. These were alphanumeric sequences beginning with *HX*. These entries were the kind used by temporary contractors or outside personnel. The very same prefix she'd heard whispered over the hunters' comms during the lockdown.

The realization hit her like chilly rain. Whoever was helping them wasn't breaking in from outside. They were inside already.

The hum of the vending machine sounded suddenly too loud. The shadows between the vending alcove and the medicine storage door seemed to thicken, as if listening.

Evelyn gathered the pages closer, heart hammering, her mind racing through faces and possibilities. Someone she worked beside, someone trusted enough to move freely through the wards.

Evelyn sifted through the logs again, her eyes darting from line to line as the same name surfaced. It was always hovering near the moments that didn't make sense. She didn't want to believe it. Clara had been part of St. Augustine's long before Evelyn's first night on the ward.

Nurse Clara Reeves was the kind of colleague everyone relied on. She had steady hands, was calm under pressure, and had an encyclopedic grasp of medications and procedures that had saved more than one doctor's pride. Her laugh could cut through the thickest night-shift gloom, her smile warm enough to make even the most jaded patient relax. Evelyn had once admired her, even leaned on her during the long, uncertain weeks after her turning when human normalcy felt like a fragile act.

But the pattern on the page didn't lie. Clara's ID was everywhere it shouldn't have been.

The fluorescent light hummed above, flickering as Evelyn stared down at the columns of numbers that betrayed something deeper. Betrayed *trust*.

She thought back to the night of the lockdown. She thought back to the way Clara had seemed unbothered, almost *too calm* when the alerts sounded. How she'd vanished from the nurse's station for half an hour with a casual mention of "checking on the generator systems." Evelyn hadn't questioned it then.

Now she could feel a knot forming low in her stomach and dread laced with a growing sense of betrayal.

If Clara was involved with the hunters, the danger wasn't just outside the hospital walls anymore. It was walking the halls in scrubs and a reassuring smile.

Evelyn sank deeper into the chair, fingers brushing over the stack of logs as if touching them could erase the truth they revealed. Her mind recoiled at the idea that Clara Reeves, her friend and colleague, was a hunter operative? It didn't compute.

Clara had been there during late-night emergencies, lending steady hands when chaos erupted. She had guided new nurses, shared her knowledge freely, and offered that warm, easy smile that had comforted so many, even in the darkest moments. Evelyn had trusted her, leaned on her, even confided in her more than she had intended.

And yet, the logs didn't lie. Every irregular swipe, every impossible timestamp, every coded access point painted a picture that contradicted every memory Evelyn had of her colleague. The notion gnawed at her that betrayal wasn't supposed to wear a familiar face.

Her chest tightened as guilt and disbelief collided. *Maybe I misread it,* she thought. *Maybe it's a mistake, a glitch in the system, a coincidence.* But even as she clung to that hope, a voice inside her whispered that coincidences didn't leave trails like these.

Evelyn's eyes scanned the logs again, tracing Clara's initials over and over, trying to reconcile the evidence with the person she knew. She felt like she was staring down a fissure that could split her world in two: one side holding the comfort of trust, the other the icy certainty of betrayal.

A faint hum from the hall echoed through the lounge, and Evelyn flinched, the storm outside matching the turmoil inside her chest. She wasn't ready to act yet; not while her disbelief fought against the weight of proof.

Her hands tightened into fists. *If Clara is really involved... I have to be ready.*

The lounge door creaked open, and Mateo stepped in first, his usual easy grin lighting up even the dim, flickering emergency lights. "Storm's really hitting tonight," he said, shaking water from his coat. "I swear the wind's trying to blow the whole roof off."

Dr. Kwon followed close behind, her expression sharp beneath the flicker of candlelight. "And yet here we are, still manning the fort," she said, her voice calm but tinged with urgency. She glanced around the lounge, taking in the half-empty coffee cups and scattered paperwork.

Evelyn quickly slid the stack of logs back toward the center of the table, covering the evidence she'd just discovered. Her chest still hummed with the tension of betrayal, and she clenched her jaw to keep it from spilling into her tone.

"Everything secure?" Dr. Kwon asked, raising an eyebrow as she leaned against the counter.

"For now," Evelyn replied, forcing a casual edge into her voice. She kept her eyes away from the corner of the table where Clara's name lingered in ink, her mind replaying the impossible possibility.

Mateo tossed a damp towel onto the counter, shrugging. "The lockdown's a bit overkill, don't you think? I mean, come on, it's a hospital, not a bank vault."

Evelyn forced a short laugh. "Better safe than sorry," she said, though her pulse quickened at the thought that the danger might already be inside these walls.

Dr. Kwon's gaze swept the room, pausing on Evelyn for a heartbeat longer than usual. "The storm's affecting the generators too. Keep an eye on the monitors," she said. "And stay alert. Something about tonight… doesn't sit right with me."

Evelyn nodded, swallowing the lump of fear rising in her throat. She smiled lightly at Mateo's playful comment, masking the turmoil gnawing at the edges of her thoughts. The logs were there, hidden in plain sight, and the knowledge of betrayal simmered beneath the surface, a secret she couldn't yet share.

The storm roared outside, the lights flickered again, and the three of them stood in uneasy camaraderie, unaware of just how close the hunters and the traitor in their midst had come.

The door swung open again with a quiet hiss, and Clara Reeves stepped in, shaking droplets of rain from her ponytail. Her scrubs were pristine despite the chaos of the night, her ID badge catching the flicker of emergency light as she smiled.

"Feels like the world's ending out there," she said lightly, brushing a stray lock of hair from her forehead. "Generators are groaning, half the halls are dark, and the ER's a circus. I'm starting to think this place is held together by caffeine and stubbornness."

Mateo chuckled, reaching for his thermos. "You say that like it's a bad thing."

Dr. Kwon glanced at her watch, muttering something about checking on the surgical wing. "If the world *is* ending," she said dryly, "I'd at least like it properly documented. Keep an eye on things, will you?"

She gave Evelyn a brief, knowing look of half-trust and half warning before slipping out. Mateo followed, humming under his breath, tossing a wink at Clara. "Try not to burn the place down while I'm gone."

That left Evelyn and Clara alone.

The lounge fell into the steady hum of the generator, punctuated by the patter of rain against the windows. Clara crossed to the counter, pouring herself a cup of stale coffee, her movements calm, practiced, *normal.* She leaned against the counter, hands wrapped around the cup for warmth.

"Long night, huh?" she said, her tone friendly, unbothered. "Lockdowns always make people twitchy. You'd think after all the drills we've done, we'd be used to it by now."

Evelyn forced a smile, though her pulse thrummed with unease. The woman before her looked exactly as she always had: confident, warm, and competent. There was no trace of deceit in her eyes, no hint of malice in her tone.

Still, the memory of those duplicate access logs burned in Evelyn's mind like embers beneath the surface. Every casual word, every relaxed gesture, felt rehearsed.

She leaned forward slightly, pretending to straighten the stack of papers on the table, masking her tremor with motion.

"Yeah," Evelyn said softly. "You'd think."

Clara's smile didn't falter, but something in her gaze flickered gone before Evelyn could name it.

Evelyn's heartbeat drummed in her ears, a slow, heavy rhythm she could almost taste. The air between her and Clara thickened into a taut, electric silence. She couldn't hold it in any longer.

"Clara," she said quietly, rising from her chair, "how long have you been working night shift security rotations?"

Clara blinked, caught off guard. "Excuse me?"

Evelyn stepped closer, voice low but steady. "The access logs. They've been altered. Someone's been letting people in during restricted hours. People who shouldn't *be here*."

For a moment, Clara's easy smile returned, that gentle mask of confusion. "Evelyn, you've been under a lot of stress lately. With the lockdown, the power outage…"

"Don't," Evelyn snapped, sharper than she intended. "Don't do that. Don't talk to me like I'm losing it." She met Clara's eyes head-on, pulse thrumming with both fear and clarity. "You know what I'm talking about. You were on call every time the breaches happened. And now, tonight? The hunters are in the building."

The silence that followed was deeper than before. Clara's shoulders lowered a fraction. Her smile faded, replaced by something faintly mournful.

"Evelyn," she murmured, setting her coffee cup down, "I didn't want you to find out like this."

Her hand slipped into her purse. Evelyn stiffened, every nerve screaming.

Clara drew out a slender syringe; its contents glinted with a faint, unnatural shimmer under the dim light. The needle's tip caught a flash of silver.

"I'm not your enemy," Clara said softly. "But you're in over your head."

Evelyn's gaze flicked between the syringe and Clara's face. "Silver," she whispered. "You're one of them."

Clara nodded once, slow, deliberate. "I'm a hunter operative. I have been embedded for years."

The room seemed to constrict around them, the shadows pressing in tighter.

Clara's tone softened, the way a teacher might soothe a frightened child.

"We don't want you, Evelyn," she said, keeping the silver syringe loosely at her side. "No one does. This isn't about you."

Evelyn stood frozen between two impulses, flight and fury. "You're standing here with poison in your hand, and you expect me to believe that?"

Clara took a cautious step closer, her white sneakers whispering against the linoleum. "Listen to me. You don't understand what you've gotten tangled in. The man you've been protecting isn't some patient. He's centuries old and dangerous. He's not cursed, he *is* the curse."

Evelyn's throat tightened, but she didn't move.

Clara pressed on, her voice almost pleading. "The hunters only want him. Not you. If you step aside, if you walk away right now, no one will touch you. You can go back to your life. You don't even have to lie for him anymore."

The words hit like shrapnel, each one sharp with betrayal, wrapped in the illusion of mercy.

Evelyn's pulse thundered in her temples. "You think I'd just stand by and let you…"

"Kill him?" Clara interrupted softly. "No. Contain him. End the spread before it begins again. That's what this hospital was built on: mercy through order. Don't let him use you like he used the others."

Her gaze flicked briefly toward the darkened window, where the wind pressed rain against the glass in streaks of silver light.

"Please, Evelyn. Just step aside. Let us finish what should have been done a century ago."

Evelyn's fingers curled into trembling fists. Somewhere beneath the fear, something older and harder began to rise.

The moment stretched two heartbeats, no more, before Clara's eyes flicked to Evelyn's wrist, where a faint pulse of unnatural light shimmered beneath the skin. The hunter's calm broke.

"Then you've already made your choice," Clara hissed.

The syringe flashed upward. Evelyn moved faster. Instinct, not thought, drove her. She swept the tray of coffee mugs off the table, sending them crashing into Clara's hand. The syringe clattered away, silver fluid splattering across the tile.

Clara lunged for it, but Evelyn was already gone, darting through the doorway, her senses flaring wide. The storm outside roared through the walls like a living thing. Every fluorescent flicker, every echoing footstep down the corridor, painted itself in her mind with terrifying clarity.

She could *hear* Clara's breath two floors below as she took the stairs three at a time. Evelyn slipped into the service stairwell, clutching the edge of the railing, moving silently. Her eyes caught the glint of metal below. The syringe had been recovered, and the hunt had resumed.

Clara was methodical, trained. Evelyn was something else, driven by a will she barely understood.

They circled each other through dim wards and shuttered hallways, the building itself becoming a labyrinth of shadows and echoes. Clara used her knowledge of the hospital's layout. Evelyn used something deeper, her heightened hearing, her ability to sense motion to feel the pulse of another heartbeat like a beacon in the dark.

When Clara finally cornered her near the old surgical wing, Evelyn moved with preternatural speed, twisting the hunter's arm just enough to disarm without breaking bone. The syringe fell again, rolling harmlessly into a drain.

Clara froze, panting, her back pressed to the cold tile. Evelyn stood above her, trembling with adrenaline, eyes burning faintly red in the half-light. She could end it. One strike. One feed.

But she didn't.

Instead, she stepped back. "You should leave," she whispered, her voice shaking. "Before I can't stop myself."

Clara's gaze faltered, caught somewhere between hatred and something like pity, before she turned and fled into the stairwell's shadows.

Evelyn stood alone, the scent of silver and blood sharp in the air, her pulse echoing in the silence. The predator inside her seethed for release, but she had held it back. For now.

In that moment, Evelyn proved not just her strength but her restraint. Somewhere deep within, the part of her that still called itself human refused to die.

Chapter 13

Bound by Darkness

The air beneath the hospital changed long before Evelyn reached the bottom step.

The stairwell behind Radiology was sealed on every map and ignored by every staff member. It narrowed into a throat of cold stone. Each step she descended let in less of the hospital's fluorescent buzz and more of a different atmosphere entirely. The further she descended, the more damp the mineral-heavy air tinged with old incense and faint electric prickle of warding magic became. Lucian moved beside her, slower than earlier, his breath shallow, his curse gnawing through the last protections he'd been able to hold.

They reached the final landing.

The abandoned chapel opened like a secret wound beneath the city, a vaulted chamber carved from gray marble and circled by alcoves where iron sconces held trembling candles. Their flames flickered in drafts that didn't exist, shadows stretching like cautious spirits across the cracked floor. Stained-glass windows glowed faintly, though no light touched them, their depictions warped by time. The timeless images of saints whose faces had melted and holy symbols dulled into abstract bursts of color.

A long stone altar stood at the room's center. Dried wreaths of herbs hung above it, brittle as old bones. Beyond, a shallow depression in the floor revealed itself. It was etched with sigils that had darkened to a permanent rust-red. A burial pit once, centuries ago. A plague crypt. A place where the dead had been sealed and sanctified… and where the forbidden magic of the bond ritual had first been carved into the earth.

Evelyn's pulse thudded painfully in her throat.

She hadn't felt this hollow, this unsettled since the night she'd been forced to feed that patient to keep him from dying. His blood on her tongue, his desperation bleeding into hers, that awful, intimate moment still sat like a brand behind her ribs. The memory flickered now in the chapel's candlelight, unbidden and sharp. She remembered his trembling hands, the guilt in her eyes, the way her own fear had twisted into something she couldn't name.

And now, here they were, standing on the edge of something equally irreversible.

Lucian leaned against one of the cracked pews, his face drained of color. "This place remembers blood," he murmured, voice thin but steady. "It responds to it."

Evelyn swallowed hard, the echo of that earlier night whispering up her spine. The cost she'd already paid. The cost she was about to pay again.

Her gaze drifted to the sigils carved into the stone like a lattice of ancient lines and thorned motifs winding toward the altar.

A ritual designed to bind two lives. Or destroy them.

She drew in a breath that tasted of dust and old prayers.

"Tell me what I need to do."

She didn't let herself think beyond that.

The candles flared as if the chapel itself exhaled.

The first sign that the hunters were closing in was the subtle tremor in the air. It was a shift in pressure, like the chapel itself drawing breath in warning.

Lucian's head snapped toward the stairwell. "They've breached the east wing," he whispered. "Minutes, at most."

Evelyn's heart lurched, but not with panic. With decision.

She moved toward the altar, boots scuffing against the centuries-old dust. The carved sigils pulsed faintly, as if sensing her presence. Almost like they were recognizing the catalyst she was meant to become. Lucian followed, though his steps faltered, every movement pulling at the curse wrapped tight around him. His veins, shadowed beneath stretched skin, looked like dark vines climbing toward his heart.

She reached for the copper bowl at the altar's edge. It was the one Lucian had told her would anchor their blood. Her hands trembled. Not from fear of the hunters. From the knowledge that she was about to step willingly into something she had once sworn she would never touch.

"Evelyn," Lucian rasped. "There's still time to walk away."

"No," she said, and to her own surprise, her voice didn't break. "There isn't."

Each word settled like a stone in her chest. Heavy. Inevitable.

The forced feeding still haunted her; the moment she had crossed a line she'd never imagined crossing when survival had demanded something both monstrous and intimate. There was no undoing that choice. No returning to the woman she had been before blood had stained her lips and fear had fused her fate to his.

This ritual was just the next step down a path she was already on.

She lifted the ceremonial blade from the altar, its silver edge dulled but still humming with ancient magic.

Lucian watched her with a mixture of pain and something deeper; regret, maybe. Or gratitude. Or fear of what binding her to him would cost. "If we do this, your life will no longer be yours alone. My darkness will be yours. My enemies will be yours."

She steadied the blade between them. "They already are."

Bootsteps echoed distantly overhead. Hunters sweeping rooms. Closing in. The chapel lights flickered as power surged through the hospital above.

Lucian pressed his palm to hers, warming it, anchoring her resolve. "This will hurt," he warned. "Blood magic always does."

"I'm a nurse," she said, lifting her chin. "I know where to cut."

He huffed a breath that might've been a laugh if he weren't on the verge of collapse.

Together, they raised the blade.

First to Lucian's wrist. He didn't flinch as the blade bit in, dark, slow-moving blood welling and dripping into the copper bowl with a heavy, resonant sound.

The chapel shuddered. The stained-glass windows flickered.

Then Evelyn braced herself.

The cut burned like fire sliding under her skin, the copper bowl ringing again as her own blood joined his. Red and red, swirling, impossible to distinguish once they touched.

The sigils surrounding them ignited in a deep, smoldering crimson; responding to the mingling of life forces, ancient magic stirred like a creature waking.

A whisper threaded through the air in a language she didn't know but somehow understood: *Two paths, one fate. Bound.*

Lucian's fingers tightened around her wrist as smoke rose from the symbols etched into the floor.

"Evelyn," he murmured, voice strained as power crackled through him. "Once we start the final invocation there's no turning back."

"I know." And she did.

The hunters' footsteps grew louder. Closer. The chapel doors rattled.

Evelyn stepped into the circle beside Lucian, blood still dripping from their wrists, the magic pulling at them like a tide.

The chapel felt smaller as the ritual deepened. Its shadows drawn inward, its silence thickening until the only sounds heard were their breathing and the slow drip of shared blood into the copper bowl.

Lucian's voice shifted, becoming something layered. His own tone was woven with an ancient cadence that resonated through the walls. "Evelyn Carter," he intoned, clasping her blood-slicked hand in his. "By will. By choice. By blood."

His grip trembled, not from weakness but from the raw force of the magic rising between them, tugging at their veins like invisible threads tightening.

She echoed the words he had taught her, her voice steadier than she felt. "Lucian Deaverux. By will. By choice. By blood."

The crimson sigils carved across the floor brightened all at once, like strips of light as sharp and vivid as fresh wounds. They pulsed in a slow, steady rhythm, matching the beat of her heart. Matching the beat of his.

Heat ghosted up Evelyn's spine, lighting every nerve. The air itself seemed to thrum, vibrating through her bones, alive with centuries-old magic too deep and too primal to belong in a hospital at all, let alone beneath it.

Lucian swayed toward her, breath catching, his skin luminescent in the candlelight. "The bond is reaching," he whispered, his forehead almost touching hers. "It's trying to anchor itself."

She didn't step back. Couldn't.

The pull between them was magnetic, inevitable. It was a subtle tightening like the moment before two hands interlace or two lips meet. A wanting she felt in her chest, her stomach, her pulse.

It wasn't just the magic.

She could feel his heartbeat, which was faint, uneven, yet thrumming with a strength that hadn't been there minutes ago. Her own pulse responded instinctively, syncing to his rhythm as if guided by an unseen hand.

Lucian's gaze flicked down to her mouth before he jerked his eyes away, jaw tightening. "Evelyn…" He swallowed hard. "The ritual is amplifying everything. Every instinct. Every urge."

"I know," she breathed, and she did, because she felt it too. The air pressed their bodies closer. The candle flames leaned toward them as though drawn by the same force binding their blood.

A low hum built beneath their feet as the sigils flared crimson, shifting toward a molten, living red that cast their shadows high across the marble walls.

"Just a little more," Lucian murmured, voice rough. "We're nearing the seal."

He raised their joined hands over the bowl. Their mingled blood glowed where it touched the copper, swirling now as if stirred by an invisible current. Light sparked up from it; thin, shimmering strands that climbed their wrists, weaving over their skin in twisting, thorned patterns.

Evelyn gasped as the markings pulsed, warm at first, then searing.

Lucian stepped closer, steadying her with a hand at her waist, fingers trembling as they sank into the fabric of her scrubs. "Breathe. Let it take hold."

His touch burned and grounded her all at once. She leaned into him because she had to, because the ritual demanded it. After all, part of her didn't want to stop herself.

Their blood, their breaths, their heartbeats braided into a single thrumming rhythm as the sigils reached their peak, blazing so bright the chapel seemed made of living fire.

The bond begins to seal.

And neither of them could look away from the other.

The world dissolved.

Not into darkness but into *him*.

Evelyn felt the floor drop away, the burning sigils stretching into red ribbons of light that curled around her wrists, her temples, her heartbeat. Lucian's hand tightened in hers, and then she fell through his memories like plunging through deep water.

Wind howled across an ancient battlefield, sharp and cold enough to flay flesh from bone. Lucian stood alone amid scorched earth, smoke rising from broken trebuchets, the air thick with the metallic tang of blood. Arrows jutted from the ground like skeletal fingers. Bodies lay scattered like a blur of armor, torn banners, extinguished lives. And Lucian, younger and unscarred, stared across the destruction with the hollow gaze of someone who had survived too much.

She felt his chest ache with the weight of command. Felt the tightening in his throat as he watched a comrade's final breath leave a too-still body. Felt centuries of exile wandering through snow-choked forests, through crumbling castles swallowed by vines, through cities that rose and fell while he remained unchanged. Isolation wrapped around him like an iron shroud.

Evelyn gasped, breath hitching in her real throat but the vision didn't release her.

Another memory unfurled: moonlight reflecting on still water as Lucian stood waist-deep in a glacial lake, hands shaking as he washed off blood that wasn't his, whispering names of people she didn't know. Voices echoed through him like accusations, pleas, and promises he couldn't keep.

He had been alone for so long that loneliness became a second bloodstream.

Then the tide turned into *her.*

Lucian inhaled sharply somewhere beside her, but their awarenesses were woven too tightly now for her to pull away. He felt her childhood nights spent listening to storms from a cracked window, waiting for parents who never came home on time. He felt her quiet dinners eaten in silence, her fingers tracing the grooves worn into the kitchen table from frantic scribbling during nursing school. He felt the hollow places inside her; rooms of grief she never let anyone enter.

He felt her hope, too. The stubborn flicker she kept alive even when everything around her dimmed. The way she looked at her patients as if willing them to fight. The way she kept choosing care over cynicism, even when it hurt.

Lucian's breath broke with something like awe.

Evelyn.

His voice echoed through the shared space, not spoken but felt. Warm, startled, and reverent.

Heat rippled through the bond, landing low in her belly. She felt what he felt as he looked at her like this, fragile, blooming want tangled with fear and something dangerously close to devotion. His desire wasn't predatory but aching, restrained, threaded with a tragic patience centuries old.

Her pulse answered him, unbidden.

Evelyn reached for him, whether in memory or reality, she couldn't tell, and he met her halfway, their foreheads pressing together in a moment so intimate it stole breath from both bodies.

The bond pulled them tighter. Too tight.

Light surged around them, red, white, and gold, until memory self-blurred. Their heartbeats overlapped. Their thoughts brushed like fingertips.

You are not alone, she whispered inside his mind surprised by the certainty of it.

Neither are you, he answered, voice trembling with truth he had never dared speak aloud.

The sigils flared, demanding the seal.

But for a suspended heartbeat, there was only the two of them bound by blood, memory, and a rising intensity neither could hide from anymore.

The chapel shuddered as if the building itself were exhaling after centuries of holding its breath.

The red ribbons of magic coalesced into a single, scorching line that traced up Evelyn's wrist and forearm, curling in thorned loops like a living vine. Heat flared beneath her skin, sharp but not painful. It was more like a fire awakening in her blood. She gasped as the pattern spread, glowing faintly, pulsing in time with her heartbeat. The sigil was alive, thrumming with the power of old bloodlines, of ancient oaths, of magic older than any hospital foundation.

Lucian's hand remained locked with hers, but she could feel the bond stretching outward, connecting them in a lattice of energy that defied comprehension. The air around them shimmered, faint whispers threading through it with hints of voices, of knowledge, and of secrets buried in the centuries of vampire courts and royal intrigue.

She glimpsed, fleetingly, the sprawling web of Lucian's world: the Court of Night, cloaked in darkness and diplomacy, princes and queens whose politics could topple cities; ancient covenants that had bound vampire bloodlines for generations; and hunters everywhere, networked and patient, waiting for a misstep. The blood ritual had opened a doorway to knowledge she had never imagined, and part of her thrilled and recoiled all at once.

Lucian's gaze was locked on hers, amber eyes alight with unspoken understanding. He whispered "This bond… it ties us not just to each other, but to everything that moves in the shadows. The prophecy, the hunters, the royal bloodline… you are now part of it."

Evelyn swallowed, trembling, her fingers tightening on his. "I… I understand," she admitted, though only partially. The world she thought she knew had expanded in ways she couldn't yet process.

The crimson light of the sigil dimmed to a steady glow, like embers of a fire that refused to die. Its thorned edges seemed almost sentient, curling around her veins, whispering promises of power and danger.

And yet, amid the magic, the history, and the prophecies, one truth crystallized: they were bound. Their fates, their strengths, their enemies now intertwined in ways that would echo far beyond the walls of the forgotten chapel.

The bond had sealed.

The air finally stilled, the pulsing glow of the sigil fading into a steady, living ember beneath Evelyn's skin. She flexed her fingers and felt an echoing thrum that reached through her blood, tethered now to Lucian's own heartbeat, his life force intertwined with hers.

Lucian sagged against her, a shudder of relief rippling through him. The curse that had gnawed at him for centuries, slow, insidious rot that had claimed allies, servants, and lovers alike, recoiled as the bond anchored him. He was alive. Whole, for the first time in decades. The magic of their intertwined blood had held back the darkness, but not without leaving its mark.

Their wrists, forearms, hearts, and minds carried the evidence of their union. The thorned sigils now burned faintly into their flesh, glowing like distant stars through the night. These were not merely reminders of a ritual performed, but warnings to the world: two lives bound, two forces now linked against a tide of enemies, both mortal and immortal.

Through the haze of the ritual, Evelyn caught a glimpse of the wider tapestry of the world they had stepped into. The Court of Night stirred in its shadowed palaces, the threads of vampire politics tightening as news of the bond would ripple through centuries-old hierarchies. Hunters, both mortal and supernatural, would take notice with coordinated and relentless patience. And prophecy, whispered through centuries of crypts, journals, and bloodied ledgers, hinted that the union of healer and prince was no accident but a fulcrum upon which destiny now pivoted.

Evelyn drew a trembling breath, glancing at Lucian. Their eyes met, reflecting both relief and the weight of what they had undertaken. Each knew the cost. Each knew the danger had only deepened.

The curse had halted, but the war was far from over.

Outside the chapel, the storm raged against the hospital above, wind thrashing and floodlights flickering. Within, the two bound by blood and fate stood together, marked and inseparable, ready for the chaos that was coming.

The siege was inevitable. And now, they would face it not as two, but as one.

Chapter 14

The Siege

The storm hit without warning. One moment the hospital hummed with its usual midnight rhythm; the next, it exhaled into darkness. A thundercrack rolled across the city like a felled titan, and every fluorescent light in St. Augustine's shuddered before dying all at once. For a breath, the corridors were pitch black.

Then the generators caught.

A low, teeth-rattling hum vibrated through the walls as emergency lights flickered awake. The thin, sickly strips of fluorescence sputtered in and out. Crimson EXIT signs burned steadily above door frames, their glow stretching long, jagged shadows over the linoleum floors. The hospital transformed into a maze of half-light. Every hallway was too hollow, and every reflection in a window too easily mistaken for something watching.

The scent changed with the darkness. Ozone from the ruptured electrical grid seeped in from outside, carried on damp gusts that slipped through the loading dock doors. It mingled uneasily with the sharp tang of disinfectant and the metallic scent of fresh blood drifting from the trauma wing. Every shift of air tasted charged, as if the storm had reached into the hospital and curled its fingers around the building's spine.

Evelyn paused at the nurses' station, letting the hush of the blackout settle into her bones. She no longer flinched at the sensory overload that followed. Instead, she breathed it in, letting the world bloom into sharper contrast. The faint heat signatures of patients shimmered behind curtains. The flutter of anxious heartbeats thrummed like distant drums. Even the scuff of rubber soles ten rooms away drew crisp and clear, threading through the rhythmic drone of the generators.

For once, she didn't fight it. She didn't tuck anything away or pretend she was unchanged. She simply *was*. Every elevated sense sharpened, every instinct unmasked in the darkness.

A few rooms down, Lucian pushed himself upright from the bed he'd been recovering in. Even weakened, there was something unmistakably commanding in the way he moved, back straight, gaze sweeping the hall with a measured authority that didn't belong to any modern man. The red glow from an EXIT sign caught the angles of his face, casting him in stark relief. The dimmed lights painted him less patient and more prince in exile.

Nurses drifted toward him, drawn by some silent gravity. He didn't raise his voice, but when he spoke, he was calm and certain. The tension in their shoulders eased. Even in a blackout, even battered and unsteady, Lucian carried himself like someone born to stand between chaos and the people trapped inside it.

And in the fractured glow of emergency lighting, Evelyn felt her pulse tighten. It was not a feeling of fear, but one of growing certainty that something bigger than the storm was about to break open.

Evelyn froze mid-stride, one hand braced lightly against a wall still vibrating with generator hum. The hospital around her was restless with patients murmuring behind half-closed curtains, distant equipment beeping out of sync, and a nurse cursing softly as she fumbled with a flashlight. All of it layered into a chaotic rhythm she'd learned to interpret.

But something new slid beneath it.

Her head snapped toward the ambulance bay even before she understood why. It wasn't noise, not exactly. It was the absence of the right kind of noise. No frantic EMT chatter, no clatter of gurneys, no pounding footsteps rushing a critical patient inside.

Instead, there **three sets of steps**, measured and evenly spaced. Too deliberate.

Their heartbeats barely elevated despite the storm, the blackout, the palpable tension blanketing the building. No adrenaline spikes. No fear. No uncertainty.

Predators didn't stalk with racing hearts.

A prickle crawled along her spine.

She strained her senses further, letting the hospital melt away as she focused. The air tasted different in the direction they approached. The smell of fabric softener wafted from their uniforms, but then she smelled it again, that was wrong. A chemical undertone beneath it, something sterile and synthetic meant to mimic authenticity. Paramedic costumes, not gear worn in long shifts.

Her pulse quickened.

They hadn't triggered the external alarms. They were too skilled for that. They must have cut the power lines intentionally, using the storm as cover. She didn't need to see through the walls to know they'd slipped into the bay with false calm, hands steady on hidden weapons.

Evelyn felt the vibrations of their approach through the floor more than she heard them. Their stride was confident and silent. Like they owned every inch of shadow they moved through.

She drew a breath, slow and controlled, letting her senses map the corridor as easily as if it were lit. Heat signatures flared. Her vision sharpened to near-infrared clarity beneath the flickering fluorescents.

The metallic taste of their concealed steel tingled at the back of her tongue.

Hunters. They were inside.

She didn't shout for help. Didn't reach for a panic button that would already be dead. Instead, she stepped away from the nurses' station and moved toward Lucian's room with a speed none of the staff would have believed if they'd seen it. Her body flowed through darkness with inhuman precision, each footfall so light it barely whispered against the floor.

Lucian felt her presence before she spoke, his gaze lifting, the old-world authority in his posture tightening as if he sensed the shift in the air.

"Evelyn?" he asked quietly.

"They're here," she murmured, every word taut. "And they're not bothering with alarms."

Lucian's gaze had already shifted past her, toward the darkened hallway, long before her warning reached his lips. He didn't need her heightened senses to know the air had changed. A subtle pressure pressed against him. An old instinct, honed through centuries of danger, stirring like a blade sliding free of its sheath.

"I felt them," he said quietly, voice low enough that only she could hear.

Before she could protest, he was on his feet. The bed creaked in relief as he rose, still unsteady but fueled by something deeper than strength; purpose, maybe, or the old reflex to stand between danger and those too fragile to face it. His bare torso caught the pulse of the red EXIT sign outside the room, casting his skin in washes of crimson and shadow. A map of old scars glimmered across his chest. The memories of battles fought long before she was born.

In addition to those scars, the sigil on his chest and the one on her wrist were glowing with a pulse that showed their heartbeats were in sync as one.

He winced once, a sharp flicker of pain from still-healing wounds, but stifled it as he reached for the pair of black paramedic cargo pants folded at the foot of his bed; spare clothing Evelyn had brought earlier. He stepped into them with speed that belied his condition, bracing a hand briefly against the wall as a wave of dizziness hit.

Evelyn moved toward him instinctively, ready to steady him, but stopped herself inches away. Her hand hovered between them, uncertain.

He noticed.

A faint, wry curve touched his mouth. "I'm injured, not helpless."

"You're recovering," she countered. "There's a difference."

He held her gaze as he fastened the last button, his fingers brushing the waistband with a deliberate slowness that almost dared her to argue with his readiness. The closeness of the storm, the low hum of generators, the distant shuffle of the waking hospital all seemed to fall away for a heartbeat as their eyes locked.

The tension between them, which was already sharp since the night of the blood-binding, pulled tighter. It hummed beneath her skin, a magnetic thread drawing her forward, even as caution whispered that proximity to him was far more dangerous than the hunters could ever be.

He stepped closer, just a fraction, enough that she could feel the heat radiating off his bare skin. His voice dropped to a private murmur meant for her alone.

"I won't let them touch you," he said instinctively.

"You're hardly in condition to be playing shield," she replied, but her voice betrayed a softness she didn't intend. "And I'm not the one who needs protecting."

"No," he said, brushing past her, not touching, but close enough that her breath hitched. "But you are the one they'll try to take."

Her senses sharpened again, pulling her back into the present. The hunters were near. Too near.

Lucian steadied himself against the doorframe, gathering strength. The glow from the corridor threw the sharp planes of his shoulders into stark relief. He inhaled once, slow and deep, centering himself.

"Tell me where," he murmured.

And Evelyn's heart pounding with fear, fury, and something far more dangerous, turned her senses outward, tracing the approaching predators through the maze of darkened corridors.

A sharp, metallic snap echoed somewhere deep in the building. It was small and distant, easily mistaken for a breaker tripping. But Evelyn stiffened. Lucian did too.

The hunters had cut the phone lines.

A second snap followed, accompanied by a stuttering burst of static rippling through the overhead speakers like a dying breath. Every radio in the hospital's emergency network wheezed, crackled, then fell silent. The steady flow of updates, patient alerts, triage requests… all vanished mid-sentence.

The hospital became an island.

Evelyn's wrist burned.

The sigil was normally a faint, silvery mark beneath her skin that flared like molten metal, sending a pulse of heat up her arm that made her exhale sharply. At the same instant, the matching sigil etched into Lucian's chest ignited in a low, furious glow, its lines twisting faintly like something waking.

Their bond wasn't subtle. It warned. It demanded attention.

Lucian's breath hitched, not from weakness, but from the surge of ancient magic threading through him. He pressed his palm briefly over the sigil, jaw tightening as the light beneath his skin flickered like an angry heartbeat.

"They've crossed the threshold," he murmured, voice edged with something old and dangerous.

Evelyn extended her senses once more, and this time, she caught the soft hiss of the ambulance bay doors sliding open. The storm winds gusted through, carrying rainwater and the faint rustle of synthetic paramedic uniforms. Three figures moved with the smooth precision of trained killers. Their disguises were perfect from a distance, but not under *her* scrutiny. Their cadence was all wrong, too uniform, too unfazed.

They entered the hospital like they had rehearsed it for years. The hunters had arrived.

Just outside Lucian's room, the hospital staff scrambled, not yet aware of the intruders, but fully aware that the blackout made everything more dangerous.

Mateo hurried down the corridor, pushing a cart piled with IV bags and sealed instrument kits. His hair, normally styled to flirtatious perfection, was sticking to his forehead, and he muttered under his breath as he nearly collided with a gurney.

"Of all the nights for the entire grid to take a vacation," he hissed, shoving a saline box into place. "I swear, if the lights fully die again, I'm suing the weather."

Despite the panic around him, he flashed Evelyn a quick grin as he passed. It was a nervous but unmistakably flirtatious grin. "Boss lady, you okay? You look like you've seen, well, more ghosts than usual."

Evelyn forced a tight, reassuring nod. "Stay with Dr. Kwon. Don't wander."

"Wander? Honey, I run on self-preservation. My ass is staying *right there*." He snapped his fingers for emphasis and rolled on.

Dr. Meredith Kwon followed behind him with a clipboard and the kind of unflappable seriousness that made interns straighten their posture on sight. Even in the eerie half-light, she moved with brisk precision, stripping supplies from shelves and barking orders to two residents who were trying, and failing, to hide their nerves.

"We need vitals on every patient in this wing," she commanded. "Flashlight or no flashlight. Move."

Lucian watched the scramble from the doorway, one hand on the frame as he steadied himself. He looked pale, but his dark and focused eyes followed the staff with a kind of fierce protectiveness Evelyn had only glimpsed before.

"These people are brave," he said quietly.

"They're terrified," Evelyn replied.

He glanced at her, expression softening despite the tension coiling through his muscles. "Bravery is doing the work anyway."

Another flare of heat rippled through their sigils. This time, hotter and more urgent. Evelyn sucked in a breath, and Lucian's fingers flexed involuntarily over his chest.

The hunters were getting closer.

And the bond between them felt less like a warning now… and more like a countdown.

Evelyn grabbed Lucian's arm with enough urgency that he turned, eyes flashing in the dim emergency light.

"We need to go," she whispered. "You're barely standing. If we stay, we'll be cornered. And they'll kill anyone who gets between them and them."

Lucian's expression hardened. "Evelyn…"

"I'm serious." She stepped closer, lowering her voice even further as a burst of static groaned through the empty speakers overhead. "They're not here for the hospital. They're here for us. Running is the only way to keep the staff alive."

"No." His tone was flat, absolute, a wall she slammed into.

"Lucian…"

"I said no."

The shift in his voice was subtle but unmistakable. It was older than the words, older than the room, older than the storm battering the city outside. A tone carved from centuries of command, from thrones long buried and loyalties long dead. He straightened, shoulders rolling back despite the pain slicing through him, and for a heartbeat, Evelyn saw him *as he once was*:

A prince who led armies. A sovereign who did not run.

"You expect me to flee," he said, "and leave these people defenseless against hunters wearing stolen faces?" He shook his head, jaw set. "This place sheltered me. These humans treated me with care and compassion. I owe them more than shadows and escape."

"You owe them survival," she countered. "Not martyrdom."

His expression softened with something dangerously close to affection. "Evelyn," he murmured, voice dropping to a private rumble, "I do not intend to die tonight."

The hot and insistent bond beneath his skin pulsed again. It was echoing the throb at her wrist. It made her pulse stutter, made her breath catch, made the argument on her tongue falter.

He stepped past her before she could find it again.

Despite his injuries, he moved through the corridor with an authority that made people straighten instinctively. His presence gathered frightened nurses and anxious patients without him needing to raise his voice.

Mateo froze mid-rant when Lucian reached him. "Señor Devereaux? Uh… you're supposed to be resting."

Lucian placed a steadying hand on his shoulder. "Mateo. Take everyone in Rooms 302 to 310 and move them into the east supply hall. It has no external windows. You'll be safest there."

Mateo blinked. "Wait?!? you *want* me in a closet?"

Lucian managed the ghost of a smile. "Yes."

Mateo nodded, swallowing hard. "Okay. Closet. I can do a closet."

Dr. Kwon approached next, tension tight in her posture. "Mr. Devereaux, what's going on? People are panicking. If we had functioning monitors, I'd be sedating half the ward."

Lucian didn't falter. "Doctor, seal off the south corridor and move anyone stable enough into the interior waiting room. Keep them away from the ambulance bay."

She stared at him with a skeptical and assessing gaze. She then gave him a curt nod. "I don't know how you know that's the safest place in a storm, but I'll take help from anyone right now."

"It's not the storm you need to worry about," Evelyn muttered under her breath.

Lucian shot her a warning look, *not now*. And she swallowed the rest.

Patients followed his direction like he was hospital leadership instead of a half-dressed man recovering from blood loss. Something in him projected certainty and stability. An old-world gravity that wrapped around every person he spoke to.

And Evelyn watched, torn between awe and fury.

He was right. He was wrong. He was impossible.

And the hunters were getting closer.

A sharp thud echoed from the far end of the corridor, followed by another. Not the stumbling chaos of an accident. Not the startled cry of someone slipping in the dark. These were brutal and final.

Evelyn and Lucian snapped their heads toward the sound at the same instant.

The security team had reached the ambulance bay with two guards who had sprinted toward the entrance the moment the power failed, flashlights raised, radios crackling with dead static. Evelyn had heard them minutes earlier, whispering anxiously but bravely about checking the generators and securing the doors.

Now she heard nothing at all.

No footsteps. No vital signs. No breath.

Just silence. Heavy and absolute.

A faint metallic scrape drifted through the hallway. It was the unmistakable sound of a body being dragged across tile.

The nurses closest to the noise froze. Meredith Kwon's hand tightened around her clipboard until it creaked. Mateo went pale, fingers trembling against the supply cart.

Evelyn's breath caught. "They're inside the main wing."

Lucian's eyes darkened while the sigil on his chest flared with fresh heat. "They're testing the layout. Mapping our movements. They're dismantling our defenses before the staff even realizes there's a threat."

"They're hunting," Evelyn said quietly.

"Then let them find me," Lucian replied, his voice a low promise edged in ancient steel.

Before she could answer, the flickering hallway lights dimmed again, then surged back with a harsh, buzzing glow. Every EXIT sign brightened, burning red against the walls like warning beacons.

A shadow moved at the edge of the corridor.
Fast. Too fast for any human.

Evelyn inhaled sharply just as the metallic scent of spilled blood reached them from the direction of the ambulance bay.

Mateo's voice cracked. "Oh god… what was that?"

Lucian stepped forward, positioning himself between the staff and the approaching darkness. Evelyn moved to his side automatically, their sigils burning hotter with every heartbeat.

From the end of the hall, a voice echoed through the shadows.

"Found you."

The lights guttered. The hunters advanced.

And the siege of St. Augustine's truly began.

Chapter 15

Choice of the Veil

The generators died with a strangled and abrupt choking sputter that cut through the ICU like a gasp. Then the world went black.

For a heartbeat, the silence was absolute. No monitors. No soft mechanical beeps. No electrical hum beneath the floor.

Just darkness, thick and suffocating.

A jagged fork of lightning split the sky outside the windows, illuminating the ICU with a burst of stark white light. In that instant, everything snapped into brutal clarity with rows of beds of silhouetted patients sleeping under heavy sedation with curtains hanging still as shrouds. Shadows clawed up the walls before collapsing back into pitch-black.

Another flash followed, then another as the storm tightened its grip on the city. Between each burst, the darkness returned heavier, pressing in like a held breath waiting to exhale.

Somewhere deeper in the unit, the blood storage refrigerator kicked on with a low, unsettling hum, which was far too loud now, vibrating beneath the floor tiles. Its red "TEMP HOLD" indicator cast a faint, eerie glow across the wall, barely enough to push back the black.

The shadows around it didn't sit still.

They pulsed with every flicker of lightning, stretching and recoiling, pooling in unnatural shapes that seemed to twitch at the edges like they were alive in the way nightmares were alive, forming and dissolving before the eye could fully capture them.

The metallic tang of stored blood seeped into the air, mingling with the cold and ozone-heavy breath of the storm. Each gust of wind rattled the windows, sending shifts of shadow skittering across the floor like fleeing creatures.

Somewhere down the hall, a crash echoed, followed by a choked grunt abruptly cut short.

The silence that followed was worse.

The ICU had plunged into darkness… but the darkness was no longer empty.

Evelyn reached Lucian's side just as another lightning strike tore open the sky, its cold white glare flashing through the ICU windows. For a split second, the room was lit like an autopsy theater, and she saw it.

The veins beneath Lucian's skin had turned black.

Not dark, not bruised, *black*, like ink spilled beneath his flesh. They spiderwebbed outward from the sigil over his heart, pulsing faintly with each sluggish beat. The curse crawled along him like something alive, something hungry.

"Lucian…" Her voice wavered despite her effort to steady it.

He swayed, bracing a hand on a counter as his knees threatened to give. His breath came slow, almost too slowly. When Evelyn reached for his wrist to check his pulse, she felt it immediately:

A heartbeat, but barely. A slow, heavy thud… then a long, unnatural pause. Another thud… and silence again.

Human hearts didn't beat like that. Neither did vampires'. This was something worse.

Thunder boomed overhead as Lucian's eyes flickered open, pupils blown wide, barely focusing. "It's… fine," he rasped.

"It's *not* fine." Evelyn stepped closer, her voice low and fierce. "Your pulse is dropping. Your veins… Lucian, they're spreading. We need to get you out of the open. Now."

He flashed a half-smile, strained but still threaded with that stubborn, impossible defiance. "You think hiding will stop them?"

"I think staying here will kill you before they even get the chance," she snapped.

Another lightning strike illuminated his face; the gauntness in his cheeks, the sickly pallor beneath his skin, the glow of the sigil flickering weakly like a candle drowning in wax. The black veins climbed his throat now, each pulse of thunder exposing their advance.

He shuddered once, gripping the edge of a blood cart to steady himself. The shadows cast by the blood storage unit wavered across his bare torso, pooling in the hollows between the darkened veins as if drawn to the curse threading through him.

Evelyn stepped into his space, close enough to catch his shoulders when he threatened to pitch forward.

"Lucian," she whispered, "please. Just this once, let someone take care of *you*."

He lifted his gaze to her, something raw flickering in its depths; fear, maybe, or grief, or the terrifying knowledge of exactly what his failing body meant.

But whatever reply he meant to give dissolved as a sound slithered through the hallway behind them. It was a voice, low and amused, echoing through the darkness. A hunter's voice.

Evelyn stiffened. Lucian's breath hitched in pain and fury.

And the shadows behind the blood storage unit shifted again… as if something was already waiting there.

Lightning flared again, bleaching the blood lab in blinding white for a heartbeat and in that instant a shape materialized in the doorway. Tall. Still. Smiling.

When the dark rushed back in, the senior hunter remained a silhouette cut from shadow and confidence, dressed in faux paramedic gear now soaked with the storm's rain and streaked with someone else's blood. His eyes were cold and ice-pale. They fixated first on Evelyn, then on Lucian, who slumped against the counter.

"Well," he murmured. "The prodigal monster looks worse for wear."

Evelyn instinctively stepped between them, though her own pulse thundered. The hunter's grin sharpened.

"How noble." He lifted a hand in mock applause. "Half-turned. Half-bound. Half-alive. Yet still throwing yourself in front of death like you've forgotten what it tastes like."

Evelyn's jaw locked. "You don't know anything about me."

"Oh?" He cocked his head, stepping closer without hurry, his boots silent on the tile. "I know exactly what you are." His gaze skimmed the glowing sigil on her wrist. "A woman dangling on the edge of a decision she pretends she hasn't already made."

Lucian pushed off the counter, staggering forward with a growl that rattled in his throat, but his legs buckled beneath him. The hunter didn't even flinch.

"Easy, Your Highness," he said lightly. "Wouldn't want you collapsing before she hears the offer."

Evelyn reached for Lucian, steadying him, aware that the hunter was watching the gesture with a predator's fascination.

"Here's the truth, Nurse Carter." The hunter leaned against a blood storage unit, casual, as if they were discussing shift schedules. "You still have a choice. Turn him over to us alive, if possible, though at this point I'm not picky, and you keep your humanity. All of it."

Lightning ripped across the sky, illuminating his smile.

"We take the curse. We end his line. And you walk out of this hospital with clean hands and a clean soul."

Evelyn felt Lucian stiffen beside her. The black veins had reached his collarbone. His heartbeat fluttered like a candle about to go out.

"You're wasting your time," she said, but her voice trembled at the edges.

"Am I?" The hunter's eyes narrowed knowingly. "You're a healer. A woman who promised to preserve life. You think taking his blood will make you strong enough to save him? Maybe." He shrugged. "Or maybe it drags you into the dark with him."

He stepped closer, shadows twisting behind him like hungry dogs.

"You can still walk away," he whispered. "Keep your oath. Keep your soul. Keep your life."

Evelyn's fingers curled tighter around Lucian's arm. She felt every faltering beat of his failing heart. Every pulse of the curse spreads toward it. Every tremor in his body he was trying. and failing, to hide.

Her humanity had always been her anchor. Her calling. Her identity.

But saving lives was not limited to human ones. And letting fear choose for her was not healing. It was a surrender.

She lifted her chin.

Her voice was barely above a breath. "I don't save only the easy cases."

Lucian's gaze snapped to her, and she felt the weight of her choice settling into place.

Not as a victim. Not as addicted. But as a healer.

As someone who would pay the price… because a life was a life.

And Lucian's was slipping away.

The hunter's smile sharpened as he had seen her resolve harden. He misread it, though. He believed it meant surrender.

He lunged.

Evelyn was already moving.

Her hand shot out, fingers closing around the closest object on the counter. It was a loaded syringe abandoned during the blackout chaos. Not blood. Not medicine.

Air.

A full barrel of it.

The hunter's eyes widened a fraction of a second before she drove the needle into the side of his neck and slammed the plunger home.

The effect was immediate.

He staggered back, grabbing for the syringe as it dangled grotesquely from his throat. A wet, choking sound bubbled in his lungs as he clawed at his neck, eyes bulging wide with horror. His breath hitched, then gurgled as the embolism ruptured through the artery.

"You… little…" he choked, but the words died in a violent cough.

Lightning burst outside the windows again, illuminating the blood lab as the hunter collapsed to his knees. He writhed and spasmed, one hand scrabbling across the tile for purchase while the other clutched at his neck where the air was already tearing through his circulatory system like a bomb.

His last sound was a guttural, drowning groan.

Then he toppled forward onto the floor; motionless, twitching only once before going limp.

Evelyn stood over him, chest heaving, the empty syringe still clenched in her trembling hand. The storm thundered like approval. The shadows rippled around her like they, too, recognized the shift inside her.

This was not the act of someone clinging to the familiar safety of humanity.

This was the act of someone choosing.

Her choice.

Lucian swayed behind her. She turned, caught him before he slid to the ground. His skin was cold, and the black veins had reached his throat. His heartbeat was a faint, sluggish flutter against her palm.

"Evelyn…" he rasped, voice barely more than a dying exhale.

"I've got you." Her voice was firm. Fierce. Steady.

She hooked his arm over her shoulder and dragged him toward the door. Every step was agony for him, but he moved with her, trusting her without hesitation.

The shadows in the blood lab stretched behind them like fingers reaching for their retreating forms, but they didn't look back.

Evelyn tightened her grip around Lucian's waist.

She had made her choice.

Not out of desperation. Not out of fear. But out of agency, and love she was not ready to name aloud.

She chose Lucian.

And she would pay whatever price came next.

Evelyn dragged Lucian down the dim hall, her footsteps echoing in the near-dark as lightning flashed through the ICU windows. The supply closet, the only room in this wing with reinforced interior walls, waited at the far end of the corridor like a lifeboat in a sinking ship.

Lucian stumbled once, a harsh swallow jolting through him. She tightened her grip around his waist.

"Stay with me," she whispered.

He tried to answer, but only a rasp escaped. His pulse against her shoulder thudded weakly; slower… slower still. Every few steps, she felt his legs threaten to give. His body was failing. The curse was accelerating. The black veins had begun to snake over his jawline, stark against his pallor.

But his eyes remained locked on her face with something fierce and astonished burning inside them.

Lightning cracked, illuminating the hallway just long enough for Evelyn to spot the supply closet door. She lunged for it, shouldering her weight into Lucian's side to keep him upright.

Behind them, a metal groan reverberated through the ward.

The reinforced doors at the entrance. Something slammed into them. Hard.

Evelyn's heart seized. "They're breaching."

Lucian's grip on her arm tightened, not with panic but with the conviction of someone who'd seen countless battles and rarely survived them. "Evelyn… leave me. You can still…"

"No," she snapped, voice cutting through the thunder.

She shoved the closet door open with her free hand, practically hauling Lucian inside. He collapsed onto his knees as she swung the door shut behind them and engaged the manual lock. Then she grabbed the heaviest shelving unit and began dragging it across the floor.

Lucian stared at her, breath shallow, disbelief flickering over his features. "You're barricading…"

Another crash boomed down the hall. The reinforced doors shuddered under the assault.

"The hunters," Lucian finished, voice almost awed.

Evelyn braced her shoulder against the shelving, grunting as she shoved it firmly into place. The metal scraped across the tile until it slammed against the door, sealing them in.

Something slammed into the main ward doors again. A crack split through the reinforced frame. The hunters were nearly through.

Inside the tiny room, shadows swayed with every flash of lightning slicing through the single narrow window. Shelves of supplies towered around them. The gauze, saline, blood kits, and IV tubing were like silent, sterile sentinels.

Evelyn turned back to Lucian, breath ragged.

He stared up at her with an expression she had never seen on him. It wasn't command, nor was it intimidation. It wasn't even that old-world gravity he wielded like a sword.

But recognition. Respect. Something deeper. Something fragile.

"You moved like a warrior," he murmured. "And you didn't flinch."

"You needed me," she said simply.

He let out a broken sound, half a breath, half a confession, before his body swayed again. She dropped to her knees beside him, steadying him as the black veins pulsed.

Outside, the reinforced doors gave a tortured screech.

Inside, Lucian's gaze stayed locked on hers.

"You're not my subordinate," he whispered, voice thin but certain. "You never were."

Her breath hitched.

"You're my equal."

Another slam. A crack. A roar of splintering metal.

Evelyn curled her hand around his cheek, grounding him.

His next words trembled on the edge of breaking.

Because the hunters were nearly through.

And Lucian was out of time.

A deafening crash tore through the hallway outside. The reinforced doors shrieked as they buckled inward, metal warping like tinfoil under inhuman force.

Evelyn flinched, instinctively pressing closer to Lucian as dust sifted down from the closet ceiling. The hunters' voices filtered through the crack in the ward door, low and eager, vibrating with the thrill of the kill.

They were moments away.

Lucian sagged forward, catching himself against a lower shelf. The black veins crawling across his skin pulsed once, violently, before spreading further up his throat. His lips had lost almost all color. His breath hitched in long, agonizing pauses.

"Lucian… stay awake… look at me…" Evelyn gripped his shoulders, fear burning sharp in her chest.

He lifted his head. Barely. Lightning flashed behind him, carving his face into stark lines.

"There's… no time," he whispered.

The hunters slammed against the last barrier outside. The sound reverberated through the closet walls, sharp enough to make their supply shelves tremble.

Evelyn leaned in, her forehead nearly touching his. "Tell me what to do."

Lucian inhaled a slow and ragged breath as if each breath was a question his body might refuse to answer.

"The curse," he rasped. "It's… accelerating."

She didn't need him to say it. She could *see* it consuming him, inch by inch.

"It will… kill me," he whispered, "unless… unless the binding is completed."

Her heartbeat stuttered. "Complete?"

His gaze locked on hers like a fierce, unblinking laser despite the pain flooding him.

"My blood," he said hoarsely. "Taken freely. Shared willingly. It would tether us… stabilize the curse in me." His voice cracked. "In you."

Evelyn felt the ground tilt beneath her. "Lucian…"

"But there's more." His hand trembled as he reached for hers, cold fingers curling around her wrist where her sigil burned like a molten brand. "It won't just save me. It will change you. Permanently."

Her throat tightened.

"And if you refuse…" His eyes softened with a grief so profound it carved through the storm's fury. "I won't survive the night."

Another violent crash shook the door outside. A hinge snapped, flying across the hallway with a metallic clang.

Evelyn's pulse pounded in her ears. The hunters were steps away. Seconds.

Lucian gripped her hand with the last of his strength, pulling it weakly toward the darkened veins at his throat.

"My life," he whispered, voice trembling. "My curse. My blood." A beat. A plea.

"Evelyn… let me live. Let *us* live."

The closet door shuddered under the next impact, bending inward.

She had no time left.

Her decision hung between them, suspended in the heartbeat before the hunters tore through the last barrier.

Lightning strobed through the narrow window, throwing harsh, fractured light across the tiny closet. Evelyn's shadow stretched long over the shelves; Lucian's hunched form flickered in and out of view like a dying flame.

His blood darkened beneath his skin, racing toward his heart. His pulse fluttered. Stopped. Started again, each beat weaker than the last.

"Evelyn…" He breathed her name like a prayer unraveling.

Another impact slammed into the closet door. Metal bent inward, a long crack splitting through the center. Dust rained down. Supplies rattled on their shelves.

She flinched but didn't look away from him.

Her humanity. Her oath. Her calling.

The choices surged through her, clashing so fiercely she could barely breathe.

If she kept her humanity, Lucian would die.

If she saved him, she crossed a threshold she could never return from.

Her hands trembled. She pressed them against her thighs to steady them, but the shivers kept coming, running up her arms, through her chest, into her skull.

Humanity meant warmth. It meant sunlight. It meant the life she'd built with her own two stubborn hands.

Immortality meant darkness. It meant blood. It meant a world she didn't understand, bound to a man she felt far too much for.

The door outside buckled again. A hunter snarled through the widening gap.

Her heart hammered. Her breath hitched.
Lucian swayed, nearly collapsing, only held upright
by her grip on him.

And then something rose inside her.

Not fear. Not instinct. Not the echo of the curse
burning on her wrist.

But memory.

The little boy she revived after a drowning accident.
The elderly woman whose hand she held as she
fought for breath. The teenage girl, bleeding out after
a crash, whispered, "Don't let me die," while Evelyn's
own hands shook.

The countless lives she had saved. The lives she had
been *called* to save.

Her oath wasn't about humanity. It was about
healing.

About choosing life even when the cost was high.

She looked at Lucian. Truly looked. At the man
behind the prince, behind the curse, behind the
centuries of guilt and survival. A man who had fought
beside her, trusted her, and bared his fear only to her.

He wasn't asking her to surrender herself.

He was asking her to choose them both.

Her breath steadied.

"Lucian," she whispered, cupping his jaw as the hunters broke another foot of the door. "I know what I have to do."

His eyes widened, aching with a hope he was terrified to believe in.

Evelyn rose to her knees, steadying him as the last hinge tore free behind them.

"I'll save you," she murmured, voice clear now. "I'll save *us*."

The door erupted inward.

And Evelyn made her choice.

Chapter 16

The Prophetic Mark

The moment Evelyn's lips touched his skin, the storm outside seemed to shatter.

Crimson lightning tore across the sky in jagged, violent arcs that were as red as fresh blood and bright enough to paint the entire ICU in pulsing strokes. The shattered windowpane beyond the supply closet caught each flash, fracturing the light into shards that scattered across the floor in trembling reflections. Every gleam danced over spilled blood, broken glass, and toppled equipment, turning the chaos into something almost ritualistic.

Evelyn felt the first rush of his blood like fire threading through her veins.

Lucian jerked under her, a strangled sound ripping from his throat as the sigil over his heart ignited. Gold flared outward from the center, then deepened into scarlet, pulsing in time with a heartbeat that suddenly thundered back into motion. The light spilled across his chest in radiant ancient patterns that were alive with unbearable beauty.

And on Evelyn's wrist, the matching sigil burned to life.

It didn't glow softly. It *blazed* like a molten brand unfurling beneath her skin, spiraling outward in luminous veins that crawled up her arm and illuminated the cramped closet in a fever-bright glow. The gold met the scarlet, flickered, then fused into a single molten hue.

Lucian's breath caught.

Not from pain. Not from weakness.

But from the stark, unguarded vulnerability in realizing that for the first time in centuries someone else held his life between their teeth.

His hand lifted, trembling, brushing a strand of hair from Evelyn's face as if afraid she might break, or disappear, or become something he hadn't earned the right to witness. His voice cracked with something raw, something reverent.

"Evelyn…"

She didn't stop. Couldn't stop.

The taste of his blood ignited every nerve inside her, unraveling the edges of her humanity not with darkness, but with clarity. A rising sense of who she was becoming and what she was crossing into. It rippled through her in waves. It wasn't horror. It wasn't a loss.

It was awakening.

With each swallow, the storm answered with crimson lightning clawing across the clouds, rattling the building's bones. Every pulse of the sigil sent sparks through her limbs, carrying an ancient rhythm she had never known how to listen for until now.

Her new senses reached outward with flickers of distant heartbeats, the thunder of pulse against throats five rooms away, the tremor of life-force leaking through walls and floors and broken doors. It was too much, but she didn't recoil.

She *opened.* Leaned in. Allowed the veil she had clung to her entire life to peel back, revealing everything she had been terrified to see.

Lucian pulled her closer, forehead pressed to hers. His voice trembled against her mouth.

"You shouldn't… this should never have been your burden."

Lightning roared, drowning his words in the storm's fury.

But Evelyn heard him regardless. Not with ears but *with blood.*

And she whispered against his skin. Her steady and certain breath was warm on his pulse.

"It's not a burden. It's who I'm choosing to become."

Another crimson bolt split the sky, shaking the building. Somewhere beyond the closet, alarms sputtered back to life. Shadows convulsed in the hall like struck beasts.

Magic vibrated through the walls.

The air inside the ICU shifted. First, there was a tremor, then a low, resonant pulse that rolled through the floors and walls like a heartbeat awakening in the bones of the building itself.

Evelyn felt it before she saw it.

The walls inhaled.

Not literally. Not with lungs or breath, but with a swell of ancient energy that expanded outward, rippling the shadows along the corridor. Cracks in the plaster glowed faintly, as if veins of light were threading through them. Curtain rods rattled. Hanging IV bags quivered. The very structure of St. Augustine's seemed to *respond* to the blood-drinking and to the magic, tearing open the fabric of the mundane world.

Lucian lifted his head, eyes widening. "The veil…" he whispered. "It's thinning."

A roar echoed down the hall as a hunter staggered backward into the flickering emergency lights, clutching his face.

Smoke sizzled from his skin.

The walls pulsed another beat of that rising, ancient power and the hunter shrieked as if struck by fire. Two more hunters skidded away from the closet door, recoiling from the glowing sigils radiating from Evelyn and Lucian like halos carved from flame.

Lightning crashed outside. A wave of gold-scarlet light burst from Evelyn's wrist, winding up her arm and out through her fingertips. When she stepped forward, the glow flared brighter, casting her silhouette long and sharp across the hall.

Lucian rose with a steady determination now, breathing hard but alive; his own sigil blazing in perfect harmony.

The nearest hunter lunged.

Evelyn didn't think.

She moved.

Her body responded with fluid precision she had never been taught and never trained for. Instinct merging with power. She parried the blow, twisting aside with preternatural speed, her hand catching the hunter's wrist. A surge of raw energy burst from her skin, knocking him back so violently that he slammed into the wall hard enough to dent metal.

She stared at her hands, stunned for all of one second.

Lucian's voice pulled her back. "Don't hesitate."

She didn't.

A second hunter charged from her right, blade raised. Evelyn pivoted, sweeping her leg out. He went airborne with a crash into a rolling vital-signs monitor that exploded into sparks. The crimson lightning outside flared again, its reflection running like blood along the floor as she advanced.

This time, she *chose* to strike.

Her palm met the hunter's chest.

A burst of gold-scarlet light erupted from her touch, searing a mark into his armor. He shrieked, stumbling back, smoke rising from the wound as though he had touched consecrated fire.

Lucian moved with her, fighting beside her. Equal. Matched. Bound.

The walls pulsed again, breathing alive and energy that exploded out of nowhere.

Evelyn spun to face the last two hunters cornering the corridor. She felt neither fear nor doubt. For the first time, the veil between who she had been and who she was becoming didn't feel like a line she was crossing.

It felt like a *doorway opening*.

This wasn't a loss.

This was a transformation.

This was power fused with purpose. Hers to wield, not to fear.

She met the hunters' gaze, her voice low and unrecognizable even to herself.

"You shouldn't have come here."

The hunters attacked as one.

Gold and scarlet light exploded down the hall as Evelyn and Lucian surged forward together.

And for the first time all night, the hunters began to fall back.

The last of the hunters dropped to one knee, clutching the burn seared across his chest where Evelyn's hand had struck him. Smoke curled from the wound; gold-scarlet light still shimmered faintly along his armor, eating through the plating like acid. He stared up at her with something she never expected to see in a hunter's eyes.

Fear.

The others were already down, some unconscious, some scrambling backward on trembling legs, trying to escape the burning pressure radiating from Evelyn and Lucian. The hallway smelled of ozone, scorched metal, and a strange sweetness like old magic brought unwillingly into the present.

Evelyn took a step forward. The hunters flinched as one.

But she didn't strike again. Not out of mercy, but because she didn't need to.

The hospital itself pulsed with another slow "breath." Light rippled across the tile in a faint, glowing wave. The walls vibrated softly, as if the ancient magic Lucian once spoke of, the old laws that bound his kind, were awakening to acknowledge the bond they had forged.

Behind her, Lucian exhaled sharply. She turned. And froze.

The black veins that had spidered across his skin were retreating.

Slowly, like ink pulled back into a quill, they unwound from his throat and chest, sinking deeper into his skin until they faded to faint shadows beneath the sigil. His dark and sharp eyes were more alive. They watched her with a wonder so open it made her breath catch.

"Evelyn," he murmured, voice steadier than it had been in hours. "It's unwinding. The curse… It's loosening."

Lightning flashed outside, but this time it was white, no longer echoing the crimson fury of the feeding. The storm was beginning to normalize.

But the bond between them was not.

Lucian stepped toward her, still breathing hard, but upright… *alive*. The sigil over his heart glowed gently, pulsing in time with hers. For the first time, he wasn't leaning on a wall. He wasn't hiding his exhaustion. He wasn't giving orders like a prince pretending not to be dying.

He simply looked at her.

And what she saw in his eyes nearly buckled her knees.

Not gratitude. Not relief. Not that tight-lipped sense of indebtedness he'd always worn like armor.

But recognition. Respect. A dawning understanding that terrified and steadied him in equal measure:

She wasn't just his healer. Or his savior. Or the woman fate had entangled him with.

She was *his equal.*

Lucian reached for her slowly, as if touching something sacred. His fingers brushed her cheek, trembling with the weight of everything unspoken.

"You stood with me," he whispered. "Not behind me."

Evelyn leaned into his touch without hesitation. "So did you."

He let out a soft, broken laugh. "I don't deserve…"

"You do," she cut in softly. "And this time, you don't get to argue."

His hand slid to her jaw, thumb tracing the edge of the glowing sigil on her wrist. He swallowed hard.

"You share my strength now," he said quietly. "You share my curse. My life. Everything that I am."

"And?" she asked, breath catching.

"And I..." He hesitated over the terrifying vulnerability of being known. "I no longer walk this path alone."

Evelyn and Lucian embraced in a long slow kiss that seemed to linger as the remaining hunters limped away into the shadows. The pair had beaten them, and wary, the hunters gave them a wide berth. The hallway fell still again, lit only by the soft hum of emergency lights and the fading pulse of magic in the walls.

Evelyn took Lucian's hand.

And the curse continued to unwind gold and scarlet light, weaving from his chest to her wrist, binding them in a rhythm older than the storm still raging outside.

The hallway settled into a trembling quiet, the kind that follows disaster but isn't quite ready to trust the silence. The scorched scent of magic and hunter still lingered in the air, mingling with antiseptic and adrenaline. Evelyn felt Lucian's hand in hers, warm now, not death-cold, and the pulsing, half-unwound curse thrummed between their skin like a second heartbeat.

Slowly, the hospital began to stir.

A door creaked open down the corridor.

Mateo peeked out first, eyes wide, hair disheveled, a clipboard held like a shield. He froze at the sight of the fallen hunters and the faint gold-scarlet glow radiating from Evelyn and Lucian.

"Uh…" Mateo blinked. Twice. "Is it safe, or should I… find a bigger closet?"

Despite everything, Evelyn's lips twitched. "It's safe."

Another door cracked open and then another. Nurses emerged, trembling but intact, their flashlights flickering weakly. Dr. Meredith Kwon stepped into the hall with practiced composure, though her eyes widened at the sight of scorched walls and the collapsed hunters.

"What in God's name happened?" she whispered, breathless.

Evelyn opened her mouth but the truth lodged in her throat. She couldn't tell them about curses and ancient marks and magic breathing through the walls.

But she didn't need to.

The staff approached, cautious but drawn by something they couldn't name. Perhaps it was the soft glow of the sigils, or the strange hush that had settled over the storm-battered unit. A few patients stepped out behind the nurses, clutching blankets and IV poles, blinking at the devastation like sleepwalkers waking from a nightmare.

Lucian straightened beside her, his posture steady, his expression calm. He looked alive. More alive than she had ever seen him. But the curse still worked beneath his skin. She could sense it, feel it. The black veins were gone, yes, but faint shadows of them still lingered like ghosts waiting for their moment.

It wasn't over. Not yet.

But the staff didn't see the lingering danger. They saw the man who had rallied them earlier. The man who stood now with Evelyn at his side, bloodstained but unbroken.

Mateo stepped closer, lowering his makeshift clipboard weapon. "You two… did this?"

Evelyn swallowed, glancing briefly at Lucian. The gold-scarlet light reflected in his eyes, softening the sharpness there.

"We protected the hospital," she said simply.

Dr. Kwon let out a breath she seemed to have been holding for hours. "Thank God you're both…" She hesitated, her gaze taking in Lucian's bare torso, the glowing sigil, Evelyn's blazing wrist. Her voice dipped. "All right."

More staff gathered, forming a loose semicircle around them. Some whispered. Some cried in relief. A few knelt beside injured hunters to restrain them, their hands steady even as they cast nervous glances at the strange symbols lighting the hall.

Evelyn felt something loosen in her chest; something old and heavy she didn't realize she had been carrying. The veil she feared crossing had not stolen anything from her. If anything, it sharpened her purpose.

These were her people. Her calling. Her responsibility.

Lucian watched the staff emerge from hiding, awe softening his features. For centuries, he had lived in shadows, feared, hunted, and mistrusted. And now here he stood, alive because someone chose him. Fought for him. Shared her life force with him.

"Evelyn," he murmured under his breath, "look."

She did.

And the sight hit her harder than any hunter's strike.

A nurse wrapped her arms around another nurse. A patient in a wheelchair wept quietly as a resident assured her she was safe. Mateo began herding people back toward the interior waiting room, waving his clipboard like a conductor leading an orchestra out of chaos. Dr. Kwon checked pulses, barking orders with renewed control.

Messy and fragile human life flowed back into the ICU.

Evelyn squeezed Lucian's hand.

The curse was unwinding. But not completely.

A low pulse still throbbed beneath their skin, warning of what still simmered in the shadows.

Evelyn drew a breath, and the world shattered open.

Sound rushed into her with the force of a tidal wave, flooding her senses until she staggered. Lucian caught her instinctively, but she barely felt his hands; the universe had split into a pulsing and living rhythm.

Heartbeats. Hundreds. Thousands. Layered over one another like overlapping drumbeats in a cosmic orchestra.

The staff around her came first, adrenaline-laced pulses thundering in her ears as they stood beside her veins. Then the patients in their rooms, fragile rhythms fluttering like moth wings.

Then… Farther.

Outside the hospital walls. Down the street. Across the storm-battered city.

The terrified heartbeat of a woman sheltering her toddler in a bathtub. The weak, thready pulse of an old man stranded in his apartment as the storm knocked out his oxygen machine. The steady thrum of paramedics trapped by fallen power lines. The erratic, panicked racing of a teenager searching for her missing dog. The strong, determined beat of a firefighter braving flooded streets. The faint yet steady rhythm of someone trapped under debris but still alive.

Life. So much life.

Her breath hitched as the wave intensified, expanding outward until she felt the entire city trembling inside her chest. Her knees buckled.

"Evelyn!" Lucian tightened his grip. "Stay with me. Focus on me."

She tried to, but the flood kept widening, stretching too far, too fast. The storm roared overhead. Crimson lightning flared again, but this time distant and muted beneath the avalanche of human existence thrumming through her.

For a heartbeat, she felt as if she were floating above the city, every life connected to hers through invisible threads of pulse and breath and fragile hope.

Then, as abruptly as it began… It snapped shut.

Evelyn gasped, collapsing forward against Lucian as the world condensed back into her body. Her ears rang. Her vision swam. Her chest heaved with the weight of too many lives settling into silence.

Lucian held her, his voice rough with concern and something deeper. "Evelyn… what did you feel?"

She lifted her head slowly. Her eyes glowed faintly gold-scarlet, reflecting the storm's dying light.

"Everyone," she whispered. A tremor ran through her. "The entire city."

Lucian's breath caught in awe.

The storm rumbled one last time, rolling across the darkened skyline like a closing curtain.

And Evelyn Carter; nurse, healer, chosen, and bound, stood in the center of St. Augustine's ICU with the heartbeat of an entire city still echoing in her bones.

Chapter 17

Dawn's Aftermath

Dawn crept over the ruined hospital like something uncertain of its welcome.

The first rays of sunlight threaded through the shattered ICU windows, scattering across shards of glass still clinging to the frames. Golden light spilled onto the linoleum, streaking across overturned gurneys and puddles of rainwater blown in during the storm. Outside, the city was waking to chaos. Sirens wailed in rising waves, bouncing off drenched buildings. Emergency vehicles splashed through flooded streets, tires hissing over slick asphalt.

Rain still fell in a thin mist, soft enough to blur the outlines of ambulances and police cruisers gathering outside. The sky hung heavy and grey, a reluctant dawn struggling to wash the crimson fury of the night before from the horizon.

Inside St. Augustine's, the fluorescent lights stuttered, flickered, and then buzzed hesitantly back to life. Their harsh glow revealed the true scope of the siege.

A battlefield.

Scorched walls stained with the shadows of magic. Cracked tile where hunters had slammed into the floor. Blood trails leading toward the trauma bay. Med carts overturned, their supplies scattered like the entrails of some mechanical beast.

And burned into the tile in long looping arcs were sigils. The crimson-black symbols that writhed faintly at the edges, as if reluctant to let go of the magic that birthed them. The symbols smelled faintly of ozone and singed iron. Some staff stepped around them carefully, as if the marks might reach out and grab their ankles.

Dr. Kwon stood near one of the walls, hand over her mouth, staring at the charred imprint of an exploded hunter weapon scorched into the plaster. "God," she whispered. "It looks like a warzone."

Evelyn had no answer. Even if she did, she wasn't sure she'd trust her voice.

Further down the hall, nurses emerged in cautious clusters, blinking into the morning glare. Their scrubs were wrinkled, smeared with dried blood and dust. Mateo Alvarez, now wearing someone's jacket over his torn scrubs, led two trembling patients out of a supply room.

He surveyed the carnage with wide eyes. "We are *never* telling the day shift about this," he muttered, though his voice trembled more than he probably knew.

More staff trickled out of hiding places, each person pausing as they took in the wreckage. The full weight of what they'd survived pressed down on the air: shock mingled with horror and a kind of reverent disbelief.

The hospital beeps resumed slowly and hesitantly as machines rebooted. Vitals monitors blinked awake. Ventilators hummed to life. The rhythm of a hospital returning from the brink.

But the ICU didn't feel like a place that had simply endured a catastrophe.

It felt like a place that had become the center of something far larger and left its fingerprints everywhere.

Evelyn stepped over a scorched sigil near the nursing station, the faint gold-scarlet glow of her wrist hidden under her sleeve as the sunrise climbed higher.

Morning had come.

The wail of sirens swelled, growing louder until red-and-blue strobes splashed across the ruined entrance of St. Augustine's. Patrol cars skidded to abrupt halts, doors flying open as uniformed officers and plainclothes investigators hurried inside with their guns drawn and radios crackling.

Evelyn exchanged a look with Lucian. His posture had settled into something regal and composed… but he stayed a step behind her. The sun hadn't yet touched him, but even this indirect daylight crackling through the broken windows sent a faint shiver of discomfort across his skin.

She squeezed his hand once and stepped forward to meet the first investigator.

Detective Ramirez strode into the ICU, dark brows lifting in something like disbelief as he surveyed the overturned gurneys, the scorched walls, the shattered glass.

"Jesus," he breathed. "What the hell happened in here?"

Dr. Julian Alvarez immediately jumped in, stepping forward with a confidence she recognized as pure adrenaline-fueled bravado. "It was chaos," he said, shaking his head as he gestured to the ruined ward. "A gang, several of them, stormed the hospital. We think they were high. Delusional. Maybe a ritual thing?" His glance flicked to Evelyn as if asking, *Ritual? Really?* but he rolled with it.

Evelyn caught the baton, nodding gravely. "We heard shouting, then explosions. The storm knocked out the power and… everything snowballed. They had homemade incendiaries and blunt weapons. They weren't targeting patients specifically, just… everything."

Ramirez squinted at her. "And the scorch marks?" He pointed at a section of wall where a hunter's weapon had detonated in a burst of unnatural heat.

Evelyn kept her face still and her heartbeat remarkably steady. She felt a new, cold precision settle over her, as if some part of her mind stepped back and observed without fear.

"Hemp-fueled Molotov variants," she said smoothly. "We've seen similar burns on ER admissions. They hit one of our oxygen carts. That's what caused most of the blasts."

Ramirez blinked, unsure whether to be impressed or overwhelmed. "You've… seen this before?"

"Big city hospital," she said with a tired shrug. "I've seen everything."

Lucian watched her, something like astonished admiration flickering across his features.

Alvarez stepped closer, plastering on a look of deeply stressed credibility. "We did everything we could to keep patients safe. Evelyn and Mr. Devereaux," he pointed subtly toward Lucian, "helped move people to secure locations. We'd be dead without them."

Ramirez's gaze drifted to Lucian, lingering for a moment too long on his bare chest, which was now covered by a borrowed button-down but still unbuttoned at the throat.

Lucian met the detective's stare without blinking. The glow beneath his shirt, where the sigil still pulsed faintly, seemed to dim at just the right moment, as though responding to her will.

Ramirez grunted. "Well, we've got paramedics outside ready to transport anyone critical. I've got more units coming to secure the building."

"Of course," Evelyn said, offering a weary, shaken smile that she didn't have to fake. "We'll cooperate fully."

Ramirez exhaled, raking a hand through his hair. "We'll need statements from all of you."

Evelyn nodded. "Whatever you need."

As he walked off, barking orders into his radio, Mateo let out a slow exhale and leaned toward her, whispering, "Okay, *boss lady,* where the hell did you learn to lie like that?"

Evelyn swallowed.

She had no idea. Or maybe she did, and the truth unsettled her.

Something inside her had shifted overnight. Her instincts sharpened not only toward healing… but toward strategy. Toward survival. She felt a cool, measured capability curling beneath her skin. Something calm enough to bluff authorities while standing in the middle of a supernatural massacre.

And she didn't hate it.

Lucian stepped beside her, lowering his voice to a near-whisper meant only for her ears.

"You handled him perfectly," he murmured. "You're… astonishing."

Her chest tightened, not with pride, but with the knowledge that she had crossed another threshold without even realizing it.

Before she could answer, a uniformed officer shouted from across the room:

"Detective! We've got a problem!"

Evelyn turned sharply.

Because the bloodstains were still there. The scorch marks were still there. However, the bodies… The hunter bodies… were gone.

Ramirez jogged toward the officer who had called out, irritation carved into his features. He reached the corner of the ICU where the bodies should have been.

Then he stopped so abruptly that he nearly slipped on the wet tile.

"What do you mean, *gone?*" he snapped.

Evelyn and Lucian hurried after him, Mateo trailing close behind. Evelyn's pulse spiked, not from fear but from recognition. She had expected this, or at least dreaded it, because hunters did not leave their dead behind.

Not ever.

They reached the far corridor where three hunters had fallen. Men Evelyn vividly remembered: one slammed into the wall by Lucian's strike, one scorched by her own glowing touch, another knocked unconscious in a heap of tactical gear.

All that remained now were the aftermaths. Boot prints scorched into tile. Small pools of blood were still steaming faintly. Silver-edged weapon fragments glint on the floor. A hunter's tactical glove, fingers severed, were blackened at the tips.

But the bodies had vanished.

"Tracks lead to the south stairwell," the officer said, voice tense. "But… the alarms never tripped. Whatever pulled them out didn't use the doors."

Lucian's jaw tightened. Evelyn felt it rather than saw the shift in his posture, the way his shoulders squared, instinctively flickering old-world authority.

"It wasn't an escape," he murmured. "It was an extraction."

Ramirez shot him a look. "You're telling me some street gang carried off their own dead without anyone hearing?"

Lucian softened his expression, switching seamlessly into the calm, eloquent tone he used when hiding the truth. "People who commit violent acts often have accomplices. They wouldn't want us identifying their dead."

Ramirez considered that… not fully convinced, but desperate for any explanation that made sense in a world he understood. "Still, someone had to move the bodies."

Evelyn's throat tightened.

Fast and quiet were hunter signatures. Invisible departures were also hunter signatures. Erasing evidence was a hunter doctrine.

This wasn't just an attack. It was a coordinated operation. One cell out of many.

Her gaze drifted down to a scorched symbol burned into the tile. A mark she hadn't noticed before. Not a random sigil. A deliberate mark, etched with precision.

A serpent coiled around a cross.

She inhaled sharply.

Purifiers. A faction she'd only heard whispers about. They were an elite hunter order rumored to move like ghosts across battlefields, leaving no trace but ash and symbols. A faction with discipline, training and purpose.

Someone had sent them here.

Lucian's hand brushed lightly at the small of her back.

"It wasn't a gang," she whispered under her breath, only loud enough for him to hear.

"No," he murmured. "It was the army's scouts."

Evelyn stared at the vanished bodies, the burned sigils, and the precise erasure of all physical proof. A chill knifed through her.

This wasn't the end of something. It was the beginning.

Behind her, Ramirez cursed and stormed toward another ruined hallway. Mateo scratched nervously at the back of his neck.

Lucian leaned in, voice barely audible. "This was coordinated. And this was only the first blow."

Evelyn's pulse fluttered. Her chest also tightened.

At first, she thought it was fear. Then the sun broke fully through a shattered window and touched her cheek.

Her knees buckled. The world tilted.

She realized the weakness wasn't fear at all… but the first burn of daylight searing into the edges of her new, hybrid blood.

Sunlight crept across the ICU floor, almost sentient in the way it stretched toward her shoe, then her ankle, then the trembling edge of her shadow.

Evelyn felt it before it touched her.

A prickle beneath her skin. A tightening around her heart. A heat that wasn't warm, but *hostile*.

Then the beam slid across her cheek.

Her breath hitched.

It felt like a razor drawn lightly along her nerves. Not burning, but a foreign pressure that made her flinch backward as if the light itself were a threat.

Lucian caught her instantly, an arm around her waist, steadying her.

"Easy," he murmured, low and urgent. "It's your first daybreak. Your body doesn't know what to do with it yet."

She clenched her jaw, trying to breathe through the sudden weakness. Her muscles felt as if they were draining of strength all at once, her knees softening, her pulse fluttering in uneven staccato beats.

"I'm fine," she whispered.

She wasn't.

Lucian shifted subtly, angling his body between her and the widening sunlight. Even that slight intervention eased the pressure scraping along her nerves.

But a new sensation rose to take its place.

A tug. A pull. A hollow ache curling deep in her belly. It was soft at first, then sharper, blooming into an uncomfortable throb that made her swallow hard.

She recognized it… or did she?

It wasn't hunger in the traditional sense.

But a pull toward something specific, someone.

Her gaze snapped to Lucian's throat.

The pulse there, warm, and the scent she could suddenly *feel* as much as smell.

Her breath caught.

Lucian felt the shift instantly. His grip tightened, protective but wary. "Evelyn," he said quietly, "look at me."

She tried, but her eyes dragged back to the line of his pulse.

"Evelyn."

His voice deepened, anchoring her. She blinked up at him, horrified at herself even as the craving flared again, subtle but insistent.

"I don't… I don't want to hurt you," she whispered, voice trembling.

"You won't." His hand rose to cradle her jaw, thumb brushing lightly along her cheek. "This is instinct, not intent. The first daylight always triggers the blood-call."

"The what?"

"A pull toward the one who shares your bond," he said softly. "Toward my blood. It's normal. It will fade."

Her breath shook. "Will it?"

He hesitated. Only for a brief moment, but she felt the truth in that pause.

"It will," he said again, more certain this time.

She closed her eyes, trying to push back the sensation curling through her veins.

Her fingers curled into his shirt, knuckles white.

The craving wasn't overwhelming. Not yet.

But it was there.

And daylight weakened her enough that it felt dangerously close to becoming something bigger.

Lucian shifted again, shielding more of her body from the sun. His expression softened. His eyes flicked to the faint gold-scarlet glow beneath her sleeve.

"You're adapting faster than I expected," he murmured. "But your body isn't used to the sun… or the bond."

She nodded, swallowing hard. "I can handle it."

"I know," he said. "But you don't have to handle it alone."

Her chest tightened from the quiet certainty in his voice.

Around them, the ICU buzzed with police chatter, staff murmurs, and the hum of returning power. However, the world felt narrowed to just the two of them. The faint echo of shared blood thrumming between them like a tether.

Evelyn clung to that steadiness…

…just as another wave of sunlight crept across the floor, inching closer.

And the craving twisted again, sharper this time, forcing her to clamp her eyes shut as the next few moments broke over her.

Lucian eased her back from the widening sunlight, guiding her into the shadowed stretch of wall where the fluorescent lights flickered but did not scrape at her nerves. His hand lingered at her waist a beat too long with a protective and grounding grip. However, his gaze had already shifted, sharpening with a purpose she recognized.

He was taking stock. Assessing the room and calculating the future.

The last of the officers moved toward the elevators, Ramirez barking orders about cordoning off entrances. Nurses limped back into their routines, shaken but determined. Dr. Kwon organized triage in a corner still untouched by scorch marks. Mateo muttered something dramatic about needing six days off and a therapist with a liquor license.

Fractures' normalcy began stitching itself together.

Lucian wasn't looking at any of them.

He was watching the burned sigils on the tile. The precise gaps where hunter bodies had vanished. The serpent coiled around a cross.

A mark Evelyn now knew she'd seen before, in rumors whispered through the underworld that was rarely spoken of.

"The Purifiers," he murmured. "They've embedded themselves deeper than I feared."

Evelyn steadied herself fully, though the craving still tugged faintly in the back of her throat. "What does that mean?"

"That someone orchestrated this." Lucian exhaled, a breath heavy with centuries of instinct. "Someone who knew the curse on my blood was weakening. Someone who wanted to prevent it from breaking."

Her pulse fluttered. Not only weakness from daylight, but also from the clarity settling inside her.

"You think the attack wasn't about killing you," she said softly. "It was about stopping… *us.*"

Lucian's eyes met hers. "The caster of the curse is still out there. And if they planned the siege… they'll strike again."

A cold certainty slid down Evelyn's spine.

"They know about the bond," he said, voice low. "They know it's changing you. They know the prophecy is moving faster than they intended."

The word *prophecy* lingered in the air, shivering between them like a living thing. Her wrist tingled where the sigil pulsed beneath her sleeve, faint gold-scarlet light flickering in response.

Evelyn swallowed. "What prophecy?"

Lucian hesitated for a fraction, but she sensed the weight behind it. "There are pieces I haven't told you. Things my family buried… and others twisted. But after last night, we don't have the luxury of waiting."

Outside, thunder rolled again. This time, not from the storm, but from helicopters passing overhead. Sirens wailed anew as more law enforcement arrived to secure the perimeter. The city was waking to panic and rumor.

And somewhere in that chaos, a larger war whispered awake.

Lucian's voice softened but sharpened with resolve. "We need answers. And we need to find the one who bound my blood in the first place. The original caster."

Evelyn nodded slowly. "Where do we start?"

His gaze drifted to the burned sigil on the floor.

"In the places that fear the truth," he whispered. "In the courts and catacombs. In hunter sanctums and vampire archives. Someone engineered this… and they will try again."

He stepped closer, lowering his voice to a confession.

"And the Purifiers are only the beginning. Factions are moving in the dark. Old powers waking. Prophecies stirring." His thumb brushed her wrist where the sigil pulsed. "This was the first strike in a much larger war."

Evelyn's breath hitched as memory shimmered: the vanished bodies, the disciplined tactics, the wall-markings. All whispers of something ancient in her blood responded, a faint echo of a shadowed throne and a prophecy she didn't yet understand.

Lucian closed the distance between them, his forehead brushing hers, a moment of fragile stillness amid the chaos.

"We survived the siege," he murmured. "But what comes next… is the Shadow Covenant."

The words fell between them like an omen.

A presage of the storm waiting just beyond dawn.

Chapter 18

A Fragile Peace

Wind whipped across the rooftop of St. Augustine's, carrying the last cool and metallic threads of the storm with it. Twilight draped itself across the sky like a velvet curtain, the storm clouds slowly tearing open to reveal a bruised, vivid streak of red along the horizon.

It wasn't the gentle pink of an ordinary sunset. It was a deeper blood-red molten. The color lit up the sky as though the sky itself remembered the violence of the night and was still bleeding it out.

Evelyn stepped closer to the edge of the roof, fingers gripping the cold railing as she looked down over the city. Rainwater pooled around her boots, trembling with each gust. The storm had moved out, leaving behind a glistening world of buildings that gleamed with reflected crimson light; wet streets shimmered like slick obsidian veins; and streetlamps flickered on one by one, casting halos across scattered puddles.

Below, the city began to glitter again.

Cars crept through intersections. Neon signs buzzed back to life. People walked along sidewalks, umbrellas bobbing, unaware they stood on the fragile crust above a night of magic, monsters, and nearly catastrophic bloodshed.

From their vantage point, the city seemed almost peaceful.

Evelyn wondered at that indifference.

Would these people ever know how close they'd come to being caught in something ancient and ruthless? Would they ever sense the undercurrent of war threading through their streets like a second circulatory system, hidden just beneath the pulse of the ordinary?

A soft step behind her pulled her attention away. Lucian joined her at the railing, his silhouette framed by the molten red light. The wind tugged at his shirt, drying rapidly on his skin as dusk settled deeper, which was safer for him.

The rooftop lights flickered, then steadied.

For a moment, neither spoke.

The city sprawled before them, glittering as if nothing had changed. As if it had no idea a siege had taken place in one of its beating hearts. As if there weren't hunters preparing their next move, as if ancient politics weren't shifting beneath Lucian's worn composure, as if the sigil on Evelyn's wrist didn't pulse with the echo of a prophecy she was only beginning to understand.

A siren wailed in the distance, weaving through the hum of traffic and the fading rumble of thunder. Somewhere below, a police radio crackled, and a rooftop vent shuddered.

However, high above it all, on the hospital's battered roof, the world felt strangely balanced between and the next coming storm.

Lucian exhaled, long and low, the wind catching his breath as if carrying it away.

"Beautiful," he murmured.

Evelyn wasn't sure if he meant the sky, the city… or something else.

The moment held for what seemed like forever.

Lucian rested his forearms on the railing beside her, eyes fixed on the glowing horizon. For a long moment, he said nothing and just watched the city with a quiet, pensive gravity Evelyn had never seen on him. The red light caught in his irises, softening the sharpness there into something almost mournful.

"When I left the Court," he began slowly, "I thought the greatest danger was the curse on my blood." He huffed a breath, not quite a laugh. "I was wrong."

Evelyn turned slightly. "What's happening there?"

He tilted his head, wind ruffling his hair as the last shards of sunlight slipped behind the clouds. "The Vampire Court isn't a single kingdom, as humans like to imagine. It's a fragile alliance of ancient houses balanced on centuries of grudges, alliances, and betrayals." His fingers tapped lightly on the railing. "And lately… fractures have grown."

His gaze dropped to the city, watching lights flicker in apartment windows far below.

"The elders cling to old power. Younger covens think the Court should adapt to survive. And then some believe any bond with mortals," his eyes flicked to her, "is a threat to our existence."

Evelyn absorbed that with a slow breath. "And you?"

Lucian's jaw tightened. "I spent centuries believing humans were fragile things to be protected from afar… admired, perhaps, but never truly *known*."

He looked at her fully then, the dimming light painting shadows beneath his cheekbones.

"But last night," he said softly, "changed that."

The words caught her off guard. "Because I didn't die?"

"No," he replied. "Because you fought. Because you chose to stand against an army when even immortals would have fled." His voice dipped, rich with quiet conviction. "You showed a courage most of my kind have forgotten exists. And you reminded me what strength really looks like."

Evelyn felt a dangerous warmth rise in her chest. The kind that threatened to unravel her ribs and settle somewhere deeper.

Lucian's eyes lingered on hers with a vulnerable and honest look that began to embed itself in Evelyn's heart.

"I once believed the Court's arrogance was justified," he admitted. "That immortality gave us clarity, superiority." A faint, bitter smile touched his lips. "But humanity has a kind of bravery we lost ages ago."

He straightened slightly, as though making a decision even he hadn't realized until this moment.

"When I return to the Court… things will not be the same. The council is fracturing with old rivalries breaking through the surface and alliances shifting like fault lines." His expression hardened with a regal steel Evelyn had seen only glimpses of. "Someone engineered the curse. Someone orchestrated the attack on the hospital. And someone intends to use both to divide us."

Her fingers tightened around the railing. "And you can't face that alone."

"No." His gaze softened again as it returned to her. "Nor do I want to."

The wind carried the scent of rain, cool against her face. Lucian stepped closer just enough that the space between their shoulders hummed with the possibility of touch.

"I won't force you into that world," he said quietly. "The politics and ghosts, the court… It's dangerous even for those born to it." He hesitated. "But if you chose to stand beside me there… I would welcome it."

Evelyn's breath hitched.

Lucian's next words were even softer, almost lost to the wind.

"You've already faced darkness with more grace than any immortal I've known. If anyone deserves a place in that world… It's you."

Darkness deepened around them.

The city glittered far below, unaware. The blood-red horizon bled into night. And the air between them thrummed with an unanswered promise.

Evelyn opened her mouth to answer, but Lucian wasn't quite finished.

"There is… something else you should know," he said, eyes drifting from the cityscape to the storm-torn sky. "The fractures in the Court didn't begin with me. They began with a prophecy. One the elders tried very hard to bury."

A chill threaded down her spine. "What kind of prophecy?"

Lucian's jaw worked once, as if weighing whether to speak the words aloud.

"They call it the Shadow Covenant." The moment the phrase left his lips, her sigil flared.

Heat pulsed beneath her skin, a sudden, throbbing beat that radiated up her arm and into her chest. Gold and scarlet flickered beneath her sleeve like something alive.

She gasped softly, clutching her wrist.

Lucian's eyes widened. "You felt it?"

Evelyn nodded, breath short. "It… reacted. Like it knew the name."

The sigil pulsed again, responding to the prophecy the way her heartbeat responded to fear or fate.

Lucian moved closer, voice hushed. "According to the oldest version, written long before my family ruled, a healer would rise in a time of bloodshed. A woman caught between life and death who could stand in the space neither species could cross."

The words seemed to thrum in her bones. *Healer. Between worlds. Bridge.*

Her pulse thundered.

"They claimed she would be able to mend more than wounds," Lucian continued, eyes searching hers. "That she would bind the veil between species… or tear it apart forever."

Evelyn shut her eyes for a moment, letting the wind coax her breath steady. The sigil's heat pulsed with her pulse a steady, insistent rhythm she couldn't ignore.

Is that why the curse reacted? Why the hunters come? Why has everything spiraled?

When she opened her eyes again, the sky had deepened to a bruised purple, streaked with dying red light. The city glittered far below, unaware of the prophecy thrumming beneath its surface.

"So," she whispered, her voice steadier than she felt, "you think this prophecy is about me?"

Lucian hesitated only briefly. "I think the Court fears it might be."

Another pulse from the sigil. Stronger.

Evelyn released her grip on the railing, letting her hand fall against her thigh where she could feel the warm beat under her palm. The sensation wasn't frightening anymore. It wasn't the alien, intrusive pulse it had been right after the siege.

It felt… grounding, like a compass pointing toward something she was finally ready to see.

"I'm not a queen," she murmured, staring out over the shimmering city lights. "I'm a nurse."

"A healer," Lucian corrected softly. "The prophecy doesn't speak of thrones. It speaks of someone who saves lives. Someone who stands where others can't."

Evelyn let the words settle.

The life she had known had already been shattered. The siege, the blood-binding, and the surge of power that let her sense every heartbeat in the city… had transformed her life long before she'd admitted it.

But this moment was the first time she had stopped resisting it.

She inhaled, the air tasting of rain and new beginnings.

"I won't be a ruler," she said quietly. "I don't want power. I don't want prophecy." Her gaze softened, focused on the flickering lights below. "But I *will* heal. And I will protect. If that has to happen in the shadows… then so be it."

Lucian turned toward her, something like awe warming the sharp lines of his expression.

"You accept it," he said softly. "All of it."

Evelyn nodded.

She wasn't running anymore.

Whatever she was becoming or whatever destiny whispered through blood, sigil, and prophecy, she would meet it as she had met everything else in her life. With the unshakable resolve of someone who had saved lives long before she tasted immortality.

The sigil pulsed one final time with a gentle, almost reassuring glow.

Lucian exhaled, a slow, almost relieved breath.

And the air between them warmed with something that felt like gravity… drawing them closer… as the dying sun bled into night.

Lucian turned toward her fully, the fading red light catching on the faint gold beneath her skin. The rooftop felt strangely caught between the hum of the city below and the shifting storm above. Between daylight's threat and night's uneasy promise.

Evelyn felt the air tighten, as if the universe leaned in.

Lucian's gaze traced her face with a softness that didn't belong to a creature forged by centuries of violence. It held something uncertain and reverent… and afraid. Not of her, but of what they were becoming.

"You know," he murmured, voice pitched low, "your acceptance terrifies me more than the prophecy ever could."

She huffed a breath of half a laugh, half a confession. "You're not the only one terrified."

The wind curled between them, tugging at her hair, carrying the smell of ozone and wet concrete. Lucian reached up slowly, giving her time to pull away, and brushed a strand behind her ear. His fingers lingered, tracing the line of her jaw, feather-light.

Every nerve in her body seemed to lean toward that touch.

"Evelyn…" he whispered, as if her name itself was fragile.

She stepped close enough for their shoulders to nearly touch, their breath to mingle in the cool evening air.

The sigil on her wrist glowed faintly, resonating with the matching mark on his chest beneath his shirt.

Her heartbeat synchronized with the pulse she felt radiating from him, not magically, just intimately.

Lucian's hand fell to her waist, fingers skimming her hip as if afraid she'd vanish. "I don't know what we are," he admitted, brushing his forehead against hers. "But I know I don't want to walk whatever comes next without you."

Her breath stuttered. "You're not used to needing anyone."

"No," he murmured. "But I'm learning."

She touched his chest lightly over the sigil, over the heartbeat and the life now tangled irrevocably with hers. He inhaled sharply at the contact, eyes fluttering shut for a second.

It wasn't a kiss.

But it wasn't one.

Their foreheads rested together, their bodies aligned not by fate or prophecy or looming war…

…but by choice.

Something fragile and powerful, yet terrifying in its sincerity.

Evelyn felt Lucian's hand tighten on her waist. She tilted her face up, not closing the distance, waiting for an uncertain invitation.

Lucian looked at her as if she were the first dawn he'd ever seen.

And then…

Wings beat the air. A sharp cry cut through dusk-lit sky.

A raven landed on the railing beside them.

Its obsidian eyes reflected the dying sun… and the silver-edged parchment clutched in its talons gleamed like a blade.

A single, solemn church bell tolled in the distance, rolling across the rooftops like an omen. The sound vibrated through the night sky, threading itself through the fragile moment between them.

Evelyn stiffened against Lucian as the raven shifted its talons on the railing, glossy feathers rippling in the wind. The creature tilted its head, fixing them both with a gaze far too intelligent to be natural. Its beak clicked once with a sharp and deliberate clack.

Then it released the parchment.

A silver-edged scroll unfurled midair before settling at Evelyn's feet, catching the last blush of the blood-red sunset. The metallic ink shimmered like wet mercury, reflecting the faint glow of her sigil.

Lucian's hand tightened on her waist.

Evelyn knelt, fingers trembling slightly as she picked up the parchment. The seal had already melted away. There was no wax nor crest. There was only the faint scent of cold iron and smoke.

She unrolled it.

Just five words, written in a script that looked carved rather than penned:

We know the prince lives.

The bell tolled again, slower this time, echoing through her bones.

Lucian's breath shuddered behind her while the wind cut colder and the last light of sunset bled away, surrendering the rooftop to the night.

Their war had only just begun.

ABOUT THE AUTHOR

Draven is a lifelong student of history and an avid reader with a passion for storytelling. With a background in Political Science from the University of South Alabama, he has spent his career navigating the worlds of politics, journalism, and business. A former politician and reporter, he now channels his deep knowledge of history and human nature into writing compelling fiction.

Born in Gurdon, Arkansas, Draven has lived in Plano, Texas, and Hernando, Mississippi, before settling in Mobile, Alabama, where he has called home for the past 30 years. His novels, d deliver gripping, suspenseful narratives that keep readers enthralled.

Through meticulous research and immersive storytelling, Draven crafts novels that explore the past while delving into the complexities of human nature, crime, and the pursuit of justice.

If you enjoyed this book, please consider leaving a positive review on Amazon at the link below. Every review truly does help. Thank you.

-Draven